THE EKWOS QUARTET

Dearn Savage

ISBN: 9798857011294

EDITION 1.0

First Published in 2023

These stories were written for Ligia Rondon and I
dedicate this book to her.
Ligia, once you were that "Little Girl" on the horse
and forever you will be my Goldbar and my Maud.
You fly me higher than to any constellation!
This carambola I lay at your feet.
Thank you.

DISCLAIMER

This is a work of fiction. Any names or characters, businesses or places, events or incidents, are fictitious. Any resemblance to actual persons, living or dead, or actual events is purely coincidental.

Introduction

Ekwos: a Proto-Indo-European word for horse.

Quartet: a group of four.

The Ekwos Quartet: The Four Horses.

Well not quite four horses in this case, but four stories which feature horses.

Not light enough in pages to be considered as short stories, yet still not heavy enough to be merited as novels.

Just right to be classed as novelettes.

The Goldilocks zone of fiction, not too short, not too long, just right.

Novelette: a narrative prose fiction whose length is shorter than most novels, but longer than most short stories.

So there you have it, four novelettes, stories of just the right length and which feature horses.

Not exclusively about horses but horses do take on a main role, if not the leading role within each of these stories.

I myself am not a horsey person as such.

I can't declare to have sat in the saddle more than perhaps six times, maybe seven if I were to count a very stubborn donkey I once was fastened upon as a child at Blackpool Pleasure Beach.

When I say I am not a "horsey person" I by no means claim that I don't like horses. I do, and I respect them. I only mean that I don't ride often and I don't know much equine terminology.

I am not sure what the difference is between a Cantor and a Gallop, or Jodhpurs and Breeches.

If you asked me to measure the hight of a horse in hands from the ground to the top of its withers I would just give you a blank stare.

So why write four stories about horses you rightly ask.

Well my answer would be that I wrote these four stories for one particular person who does know horses, who does know the difference between a Friesian and a Hanoverian (personally I would have thought that they were typing fonts).

During my scrawling down of these tales one by one I started to quite enjoy myself, I was having some fun then thought to that perhaps I could group them together under one book, join them as a Quartet.

Why four stories you may ask and not five? When if I wrote fire then I would have had to call it "The Ekwos Quintet" and to me that just does not rolled off the tongue quite the same!

Pernickety about phonaesthetics? Yes, you bet, but to be honest, four seemed just the right number, after all, many things come in fours.

Four Elements, Four-Leaf Clovers, Four Points of the Compass, Four Seasons (sometimes all four in one day if you live as I do in Scotland) and The Four Horsemen of The Apocalypse...alright, that last one is not such a cheery example so lets substitute that for The Four Nations, especially if you are a rugby fan.

This is not the first time I have wrote about horses. If you have read my previous book, a novel I wrote called "Memory Boxes" you will know that a horse does make a brief appearance near the end. But no spoilers to be had here.

Horses have been such an integral part of our history that it is to no great surprise that there are so many equine sayings and phrases interwoven into our day-to-day conversations.

Take for example "Straight from the horse's mouth" meaning to come directly from the original source, or "flogging a dead horse" as in wasting one's time. "One-horse town" describing a small and unimportant place, "Hold your horses," as in slow down, and "Eat like a horse" referring to having a big appetite.

These are but just a few in the English language yet there are of course much more.

Horses have had an important relationship with Mankind.

We have coexisted and traveled along the same paths together for many thousands of years.

They have helps us from plowing fields to hauling goods, they have been with us in battle, and they've carried us in sports. More recently they have helped improve our mental heath through equine therapy. Can we give the same kudos to any other animals which we have domesticated on this earth? I don't think we can!

Someone once said that a dog may be man's best friend but the horse wrote the history and this is so very true, the history of mankind is carried on the back of a horse.

My inspiration for **Running Horse** was a painting I once saw which is called "Together" by a Russia artist now based in Latvia by the name Fefa Koroleva. If you were to search online for this painting after you read the story you will know precisely which scene within the tale reflects this art.

The idea of the tribal tattoo on the "Little Girl's" inner arm was taken from someone I know very well and who has the exact same tattoo, which I had imagined when writing the story. She has it on her inner forearm similar to the little girl, although perhaps not inked into her skin by the same method.

With **Goldbar & Dougal** I had actually started writing this for someone quite young who then had already experienced grief and this was to be a way to address it, but then it turned into something more.

A horse with PTSD, the unwanted and recurring memories which can control efforts despite attempts and how it does not mean that love is given any less.

Then there is **From The Horse's Mouth**. This is a story as told from a certain famous flying horse from Greek Mythology.

There are many horses in legends but I would suggest that Pegasus is the most recognisable of them all, but there are also many fabrications about him, alterations from the actual myths as to fit into the Hollywood parameters. So now, from the constellations, the famous winged horse clears up some of these distortions by telling the story of his own life and that of some others of his collaborator during these mythical times.

Then finally we have **Old Man and Rose** which again touches on grief, losing a significant other and the pains brought on by old age. The "Old Man" finds a strength to continue when he sees Rose the equally old horse every day at the fence when he visits his wife's grave.

RUNNING HORSE

The horse ran throughout the night with the little girl on his bare back.

She was stretched forward, her exposed thin pale arms clinging around his muscular neck in a tight embrace, her face pressed against the crested top of his scruff, cushioned there by the soft thatch of mane but only giving scant suspension to the jarring of movement, meagerly absorbing the jostling jolts of the rough transit over gnarled topography.

The delicately spun white cotton dress which she wore billowed out behind her like the mainsail of a boat, bulged from the fierce headwind into which the horse galloped.

Many of the red begonias which were woven into the girl's long black hair by her tribe before the flight still remained intact within the tresses of her plaits flowing outward behind her head on the night's tide current.

These same flowers had been also laced into the horse's mane, their aromatic scents of soft rose and citrus now emanated even more with the equine body heat radiating from the stallion giving a sweet parcel of aromas for the girl with her face dug in deep. She tried to concentrate on its floral bouquet despite the rising ammonia sharpness of horse sweat.

The ice which was carried on the chilling piercing wind would have surely froze her by depositing its hoarfrost were it not for the heat venting up off from the horse such was his metabolic engine.

The little girl's alabaster skin at the journey's start was flawless, the only marking was the willow like trace of ceremonial body art on the inside of her left lower arm between crook and wrist.

These markings represented a running horse, delineating the very mount she was upon now.

An outlined scored with lines as thin as ant shanks etched into her tender young flesh by the Elders using sharp thorns dabbed with the ink made from ground up ebony beetles and obsidian dust.

Now that same skin, revealed to the elements was red with a painful abrasion from the scourge of the biting crisp wind and chafed by the milling against the flanks of the horse.

The tattoo of the great beast on her arm looked as if running through a fire such was the red rawness of her skin.

The horse continued to gallop at a considered swift steady pace, as to fluctuate the speed by slowing then accelerating again would cost him precious energy.

Already his reserves were running low, his energy was almost up, he was running on pure tenacity alone, determined to get this little girl who was clamped so firmly on his back to safety.

Haste alone would not emancipate them from the dangers, he had to be prudent too so concentrated on maintaining a constant cadence.

The rugged desert floor had already lacerated the leathery undersides of his hooves with its debris of scree and honed gravel.

The thorny briers of the intervening grasslands penetrated the keratin of his soles, even despite their protective thickness which the dense organic provided.

He could feel the stabbings of serrated slivers still embedded deep, especially as they were now crossing the smoother flatter surface of the salt plains with his slaps hitting on the ground flusher.

The various terrains which they had traversed gifted unwanted shrapnel which installed deep and would not dislodge.

His hooves would be the trace of their route as well as any map could ever be with etchings and deep rooted splinters.

His chestnut hue was already now paled by the salt ashes, a stamp in the passport of crossing the salt plains, just as the burrs on his coat and thorns deep in his lowers signified the grasslands as did the shale and grit would give away his desert crossing.

* * *

The osmosis effect now from the salt was also drying out the horse's already delicates causing the thick skin to crack and bled eliciting further agonies.

But he had no time to register the pain, he had to get the little girl to the Haven as quickly as he possibly could.

The horse could hear the frenzied howls of the wolves somewhere behind in his trailing wake getting closer and closer, they were still pursuing them both at speed.

More wolves merged with the pursuing pack during the progress of their chased odyssey adding numbers to the hounding.

Like iron filings to a magnet they were attracting to the hunting horde.

Their instinctual bloodlust was triggered like the nature's berserkers that they were, to run with their rabid brethren, hailed into action by the scent of not only the blood which seeped from the horse but also the flow from the girl, her inaugural start of what would be a monthly occurrence, this first of which signified her coming of age as to initiated this once only rite of passage to be undertaken on that same evening as was her tribe's custom.

The additional enticing odours of fear and horse sweat just added to the pheromonal broth lingering on the wind trails vented from the fleeing girl and horse powering the wolves forward in the hunt.

At an earlier furlong along the path of the crossing one of the wolf pack acting solitary had got close enough to score its claws down the horse's rear legs but could not quite gain the purchase it needed with it's fangs before the horse bucked then kicked it off braking the wolf's back in the process.

Still the blood from the horse's wound tainted the airstreams as a trace for the pack to tear after.

The wounded wolf which had inflicted the stallion's injury lay miles back on the grasslands terrain, spine crushed, it's corpse since frozen with the snarl of it's last defiance still plastered ice-locked on it's face by the icy wind.

The Little Girl on the horse's unsaddled back was numbed from the freezing cold and greatly fatigued from her exertions maintaining a tight grip.

She was almost cataleptic, with instincts alone keeping her arms remained locked around the horse's neck otherwise she would fall off and succumb to the chasing hungry wolves.

Her legs held fast to the horses flanks as they hurtled onward across the plains.

Her bare inner legs were chafed such was the friction from coarse haired equine epidermis during the kinetics of the rub from the chase.

The arid dry salty dust which was kicked up from the ground bit and stung painfully at her lesions yet her grip did not dare falter.

If the horse tattoo on her inner arm could be witnessed, as it pressed tightly against the stallion's pelt as she held on, it would seem to scramble and buck too, art imitating life as the flexions of her slim spindly muscles and tendons twisted and contorted with her grappling to stay tightly perched giving a life to the markings.

She muttered incantations into the horse's ear as it ran, she uttered the appellations of her descendants going back one hundred generations in the attempt to keep herself separated from the pain, names which she had been taught to memorise then recite during her lessons with the village Shaman in preparation for this rites of passage, a trick to distract the mind at such moments, focus on rhyming off forebears in remembrance to escape the force of pain threatening to cause mutiny by commandeering the mind.

The little girl was all too well aware what would become of her if the wolves caught up, she was aware what would become of them both, her and her beloved horse.

Many other girls before her have attempted this same crossing on the back of their own equine cohorts and most now have their blanched marrow purged bones laying upon these bleak plains.

She moved her mouth closer to the velvet funnel of the horse's ear, 'Run like the wind,' she whispered like a lover into it, 'Run true and chase the moon.' she murmured through her dry wind cracked lips.

The horse heard these words spoken.

He dearly loved the little girl to whom he'd been bound to since as a new born colt.

Her kind, smiling, welcoming face was the first sight he saw when he was expelled out the tunnel into the light, she was there supporting his front legs and again steadying him when be raised himself postnatally up then gambolled his first unsteady steps.

He was so near collapse, these gentle words of encouragement from one he adored so dear gave his heart a surge, one last push which only love could drive and never that of a spur or whip into his hide.

He galloped onwards, forward as if the Devil himself was at his tail like Tam o' Shanter's Meg, and that he was in a sense as the stalking wolves were heinously blackhearted without the slightest of virtues, devils of the land.

He felt the girl's tight arms around his neck and her little heels pressed to his sides.

He gauged she was secure on his back and locked in place.

Looking up at the night sky for navigation he saw the hole through which the brightest light shinned.

He slightly adjusted his direction to keep his path align in the direction of that hole above, this was his guiding star, a much early lived ancestor conducting his route ahead.

He could not see any ground blazers on the horizon so could not gauge the distance still to travel to arrive at safety, he gritted down his teeth and ran onwards.

He had been trained for this moment, they both had been.

The Elders had watched with approval as the trainers would make him run laps around the clearing to build his stamina, then dragging felled logs tethered to him with vine cord to build his strength.

Disciplined not to capitulate or yield onto the fears which were so inherent in other.

The little girl collaborated during the horse's sharpening of skills.

As from their consecrated bond at the moment os his birth her existence was a continuously presence beside him.

Her smell to his senses was as familiar as the feel of the ground under his hooves, the caress of her dainty hands as acquainted as the passage of breaths which he breathed through his nostrils.

During their daily drills together upon his bare back she would be mounted. Sometimes with her legs astride, other times prone belly down, her head looking past his withers and her delicate insteps by his croup before the dock of his tail, a stealth formation which created at a glance a horse seemingly devoid of a rider if it's silhouette were to be seen from a distance.

She would dismount using this same position, as the horse would tenderly lower his front legs, then with rearward extension of his hind limbs to bring himself down to the ground so as the girl could step off without the need to climb down from hight.

Often they would simply lay on the grass together motionless, her head resting on his long jaw, her breaths absorbed by his nostrils and their breathing synchronised together, hearts beating almost as if one when they both entered a meditative state.

Love was always the horse's encouragement never the sting of a lash and as such love was give, the same such love he returned back in return.

She would prompt him to pivot onto his back by her gentle propellant push on his front leg upwards as he was laid on his flank.

Once upon his back she would stretch out his legs one at a time holding the bulb of his heel whilst rotating his fetlock, tightening then relaxing ligaments and tendons anchored against the bones.

The stallion's training was not just about discipline, strength and endurance, there had to be bellicose elements too as there would be predators to fend off when the time came.

Coconut husks were fastened to the trees at the edge of the clearing for the horse to practice precision aims of his rear kicks preparing to repel attacks from the behind.

These husks were also scattered across the ground as to train the horse to tumble on the earth rolling over the shells, crushing them with his great muscular bulk as if they were emulated wild dogs growling up with aggressive intentions.

These exercises were repeated then repeated again some more until they were almost second nature to him. A muscle memory, movements to be conjured up on command almost instinctual for when the need would arise.

He had been tight with the girl ever since he was shed upon to the grass.

His hide was accustomed to the feeling and grind of her when they rode.

Balanced to her weight and acclimatised to her smell then tuned with the resonance of her beating heart knowing when she felt joy, sadness or fear.

Every, timbre and tone, attenuation or appreciation of emotions and mood he could detect as she was the same with him such was their intimate connection which their shared.

The horse was born from the very best purest of bloodstock. Acquired from careful selection of warrior shire and equestrian dame.

He was only feed the highest quality cotton fruit tree bark sheared from the highest branches where the sun rays nurture their elements and the ants and crawlers could not spoil their worth.

Then anointed with a special oil every evening which was made from red berries and the milk from tunnel weeds, his coat wet, sleek with sheen.

Now he was five years old, peaked to the climax of his much prepared perfection, his time had came, his purpose had arrived, his destiny, timed to match that of the little girl's first cycle's manifestation.

His duty was to carry this precious girl, his little bashert, delivering her from the village to the safety of the Haven as was her rite of passage.

This was to be a great honour for him he could not contemplate failure.

As the moon gleamed down illuminating the way ahead reflecting its radiance off the salty surface the horse did pay attention to the ground on which he ran across.

There were a wealth of ice veneered pools across the surface of the plains, their rounded diameters just shy of a couple of hand spans but many also had much depth.

If his hoof were to tap through one of the crystal salt iced surface that was still in the state of thaw from the earlier daytime sun, then he would surely breach right through and down deep sinking one of his forequarters so as to break the bone and then the crystallised mineral rocks which shined up reflecting the moonlight, would sheer through horse flesh like sharpened blades.

If that were to happen he would not be able to continue the way forward, only attempt to fend off the voracious wolves with impotent kicks and swings of his butting head but the inevitable would come to pass, and the little girl would have failed her rite.

Speed was of importance but he had to tread carefully too, the wolves were lighter and their paws would skim atop such iced glaze without so much as a crack of the thinnest fissure.

A shock of pain fired up his right leg emitted sharply from under the hoof, he almost stumbled.

Tune out this pain he thought, remember the training, block it. Do not allow it to cruise up into the head to be registered there as a feeling he told himself. Deny it of its power.

His hooves were injured beyond repair, gory cusps on the end of his legs, digging into the dusted hard ground of the salt flats and his fetlocks crowded with thorny burrs which tore and ripped even more with each and every motion but still the horse drove himself on though the excruciating agonies, the only reward wished for with such grit was to get his rider to safety.

Once past these plains the Haven must be surely close by. Goddess Gaia guid this devoted servant true as to only relinquish my passenger at her destination and for her not to become a crimson smear on this white salt sand he silently offered up to the heavens.

One consolation since leaving the grasslands miles behind and now onward over the barren desolate bareness of the salt plains was that there were no trees or rocks for a predator wolf to stage an ambush attempt as had happened previously.

A waylaying on this open ground now would be impossible to conceal.

Earlier the wolf had waited, biding it's time laying prone on top of the large boulder desiring that the horse and rider would choose that particular trail through the thicket that the boulder on which the creature had lain had abutted.

The wolf was on standby with rear legs prepared to compact into compression like springs if it heard the signals of approaching hooves.

Then it did, they had been coming its way so the wolf had loaded it's posture in tense anticipation of its attacking lunge from height off the rock. An advantageous position with the element of surprised on its side such was its cunning.

Just as the horse's flank was almost parallel to the boulder about to draw level, the wolf had then leapt hoping to pluck the girl from the horse's back but it had mistimed not only the manoeuvre but also the height of it's launch too. Then it racked itself against the horse's rump.

In attempt to recoup advantage it dug its claw into the horse's pelt, raking in as to gain purchase for climbing up the meat to peel off the girl, and was about to bite off a chunk of horse flesh to slow down the mechanics of the action but the stallion, then skidding with the forced momentum of the attack, had kicked out his back legs like a mule throwing the beast off, then with a follow-up strike catching the wolf mid-air rupturing open its belly before batting it against the very boulder from which it had launched itself breaking canis lupus vertebras in the process.

It was a lucky escape but the horse had to be more careful.

He had felt the girls heart race in fear during the encounter but it was to slow back down once he'd regained ground and the howls behind them faded once more into the distance.

This dicing dance with near death cost him much precious energy which he could ill afford. It was a lucky escape but the horse had to be more careful.

A wolf at full pelt can run almost sixty kilometres in an hour, a horse is faster at about seventy but the horse had been running for over six hours now and fatigue was settling deep within him.

Whereas the chasing wolf pack were picking up new fresh recruits on their way as they tracked after the pair.

The girl on the horse's back heard the howls oscillate all through out the night. Fainter as they fell behind then more robust as the wolves gained closer.

She estimated from the sounds than their numbers had increased since they first got on their trail shortly after leaving the village.

She understood the horse must be exhausted, his hide was soaked with sweat, the ammonia like scent now watering her eyes but still the courageous horse ran on.

She knew if they reached the Haven the horse would not have much life energy left, she would, as she told herself many times before with tears at the prospect, lay beside her trusted companion's side and keep him company until he started his spiritual journey onwards.

He'd already proven himself back at the grasslands when the wolf attacked them. His courage and strength could never be called into question, he had earned his place to graze upon the greenest pastures with his ancestral herd on Gaia's land where one day she would be with him again.

She had been paired with him since he was born, the Shaman had consulted the holes in the sky and the gods told him that this horse would be the one to protect and deliver her safe once her time was to come.

She was there during his foaling as she held his front feet with gentleness when he came out the birth canal with a strained glide on that evening of his birthing.

She had helped him to his feet and held her ear to his heart to hear then sync with its beating tune as they bonded.

She played with him until he became a yearling then his true preparation would need to begin in earnest. Then the girl would sit below the Elders perched up on their high chairs watching the horse, her horse strengthen and assemble his mind and body for the task of carrying her safely to the Haven when the time came as her rite of passage reaching womanhood demanded her exodus from the village to the far away Haven where when once there, if successful arrived with Gaia's blessing, she would find her mate and earn what would become her name, and the horse too if having succeeded would be given an appellation at the same time, either in retirement or remembrance, until should that moment arise she would just be as girl and he as horse.

The Alpha of the trailing pack was known as Fenrir.

He was larger than the others and his grey muzzle was crisscrossed with old scars of former challenges to his status.

He was getting older but his vigour had not dimmed in the slightest, he was still very much a force with a reputation amongst the pack for his atrocity.

Cruelty radiated from his eyes like glares of light.

He, as his status, strength and determination would force, was vanguard of the running pack hounding after the horse and girl.

With spiteful malice Fenrir resented the fight the horse continues to put up in attempt to deny him his prey.

He would reimburse himself with dealing both rider and horse a slow agonising end once he caught up.

His paws stung with the salted ground now and this just flared his temper up all the more.

He would soon crunch down on the little maiden's bones which he would expose from the ruptures of her legs shredded by his fangs as the horse would watch and lay panting, eviscerated by his brethren who they themselves would be red muzzle deep within his guts leisurely chewing their way toward his still beating heart!

Oh the pain he would inflict on the pair was delicious in his mind.

They both would soon be scraps of ragged mutton on bones to be masticated by the laggers of the pack.

Soon all that would he left as a memoir that the pair once even had ever existed would be the pilled dung for the beetles to roll along the ground.

He relished these thoughts in his mind pushing his own exhaustions to the side.

The horse was exhausted, his remaining reserves had been drained miles back and now he only ran with the thoughts of the little girl on his back to propel him forward.

His fuel was love, the opposite of what powered Fenrir close behind him, only the love he held for this fragile little girl kept his legs moving forward and with each excruciating pump of the stumped and bloody hooves bounding off the dusty compacted hard ground would drive just enough blood through his body to force his heart a twitch of a stitch to keep it beating beyond this moment.

As the horse ran on he gave up more prayers to the Heavens.

Gaia I beg and implore you great and mighty earth God, the horse prayed, give me the strength to get her to safety.

I ask nothing for myself, only for the little girl's life.

Take my pelt and bones to furnish your palace but please allow me just enough time to get her to safekeeping.

The little girl on his back felt the throb of the horse's racing heart fading in its fight.

She would feel it almost falter in its beat then flutter with another hardened thresh of the hooves hitting the ground.

She felt for her horse, he was her dear friend and companion and now her only hope.

'Beloved horse', the girl casted into his's ear, 'this agony will end soon then you will rest my darling, my treasured one.

Whatever shall happen now please know that our hearts are one and will always beat together for eternity no matter if we should tumble down to finish our journey here or there.'

Tears trickled from her eyes, falling tears which even the wind did not have the heart to snatch way.

They rained on the back of the horses neck cascading through his mane which he felt with the sensitivity of a single snowflake to a flame.

My intimate, he projected in return, wherever your journey should take you my shadow will always cross your's with protection and the purest love.

Fenrir could hear the horse's hooves stamp their mark on the ground as carried by the wind from ahead, he knew he was gaining on them, his intensity increased with this realisation.

Soon my quarry, soon I will be bitting at your fetlocks and snapping at your tendons.

Once I bring you down I will clamp and tear at your soft meats and rip and render.

Another wolf in the pack raced forward almost side on now to the Alpha, its ears back slipping the wind.

Fenrir turned his head towards this chancer which had jockeyed forward.

Fenrir snared displaying his yellowing dagger like fangs. The other took the hint and dropped back a pace.

Fenrir had no intentions for another to have the first snap at the meat now that it was so close. His glory and him alone will have the honour of the first blood and the time was getting ripe, the gap was closing, he could smell the blood and sweat of the horse and hormonal scent of the girl, any time now they would be his.

The horse sensed and heard the pack closing in behind him. With every stride he was almost anticipating the jolt that would be the takedown of him and the girl.

He knew his strength was now at its lowest ebb. He scanned the horizon for any sign of the encampment of the Haven but he saw none.

How much further he did not know or if he was still aligned with the shinning light up in the sky as even lifting his heavy head up toward the ceiling of the night was a struggle such was the extent of his weariness now.

The horse worried that soon the conclusion will be forced upon them. He knew his heart would simply give out within a few seconds of being forced down, despite what plans of pain and torture the wolves had in mind for him but by then they would not be able to follow through as his conscious would be far gone but the torment that overpowered his mind now was the knowledge of what they would put the little girl through!

That was a darkness in his thoughts which he was forced to confront and could not ignore any longer.

He could not allow that.

When and if he were to be felled then he would try a roll to crush his loved little girl's skull like the coconut husks he grounded himself upon crumpling their shells into pieces during his training.

He had to make her ending fast and not prolonged at the fangs and claws of the wolves.

This was a mercy the little girl deserved, one which would tear his heart before it's final beat but he had to spare her from what would be the most foul punishment at the snapping jaws of the wolves.

May Gaia judge his heart for what he would have to do, the action he planned would be born purely out of love but he knew it would break the covenanted rules forbidding him to hurt a human especially his bonded partner such as this little girl was.

Gaia would not look fondly on this despite the circumstances and he would expect to be hauled off, not on the good journey but instead down into the realms of Tartarus to suffer the perpetuity of his horseflesh burning and to be scoured and whipped eternally, but at least in his heart he would always know the little girl had not suffered a lingering painful fate and that was a result he was more than contented to accept, he begged for that trade as such was his love.

Fenrir the great wolf could see them now, he would be in striking distance within minutes.

He could see the stallion lagging, his lower shanks bleeding out through the crusting white coating of the salt dust.

Fenrir salivated at the aroma of blood which tainted the air stronger than ever now as the final meters closed, this was going to be so sweet, he almost taste that little nymph like flesh of the girl he saw jiggling on the back of the horse in front on him. Ahhh he thought, the sweet tender meat of a child, but I will make it slow, not rip out the soft throat first but start from the feet then up, savouring the screams as the coppery smelling gravy drips from my lips and let the horse be witness to the carnage he intended upon the girl.

The horse started to stumble with exhaustion, the pain was also breaking through the barriers he put up in attempt to fend off until the task was complete, a task that now he knew had no chance of being concluded with a happy ending All that was left now was to complete his last act of love by tumbling to the ground then immediately rolling across his little companion to pulverise in order to spare her.

The sun had started to rise and the ground in front about to be soon under him started to shimmer.

Feeling his hooves slithered he realised he was crossing the wide pool of a frozen Salt Loch.

He heard the baying pack close in behind him.

He could wait no longer for their takedown to be initiated as on ice the fall would be more unpredictable and he had to be sure that his last move was to put all his weight and force into the tumbling swivel as to crush over his loved one's little skull so he slowed and tensed to prepare his fall.

Fenrir, who has also in preparation, composing himself for the vital strike to take down the stallion as he saw the horse slow up and tense his quarters.

He must be exhausted, the wolf snarled to himself with satisfaction, I won't even need to pull him down by his legs, I see he is about to fall by his own accord.

The little girl on his back had already realised before they got this far what was on the horse's mind, and now she recognised his slowing which would soon twist into a turn before a forceful fall.

She'd watch it many times before from the sidelines when the big stallion trained reducing the coconut husks to exploding shells.

She understood his reason as being mercy, the wolves would make her suffering long and drawn out.

She whispered her thanks with love into his ears.

As she knew what was about to happen she braced her head down lower to the side of horse's flank in preparation for his roll hoping the crashing down would do the job instantaneously quicker in the position she now placed her little head.

'Thank you my beloved.' she called with her head pressed to his side, 'you are my very best friend and here you protect me to the very end, a truer love there has never been.

'You rest well my love, I will petition Gaia forever if need be so that we can be together again in this next life that awaits us.'

She closed her wet eyes then clamped her head to the horses side twisting her neck towards him welcoming this quick final kindness over the enduring pain which would be once captured by the wolves at now at their heels.

Just as the horse, then almost slowed to a halt, was about to commence a twisting fulcrum with the momentum before diving down on its side there was a cracking under his hooves as the ice beneath broke.

He plummeted through the splintering crust into the waters of the Salt Loch below with the little girl still fastened tight like a limpet to his back grasping tightly to his mane, still with her head lowered.

Fenrir reared to a halt as he saw what was happening in front.

A few feet further and he would be joining that mighty beast and little rider down through that opening into the depths.

Instead of being thankful for his luck the big wolf howled in frustration, the profound vexation of annoyance that the kill would not be his after the many hours of the chase.

The freezing waters would lay claim to the meat and tripes which was to be his for the taking!

Fenrir's fury sounded across the land with a sharpness which even the frosted shards of salt blown by the wind could never compete.

Some red begonia flower petals drifted slowly down to the ground in front of the wolf's nose. Teasing remnants of what had just escaped him. He snarled and snapped at them with foul infuriation as they drifted down upon the frost at his front paws, the howling wind not seeming to whisk them into flight.

The horse and the little girl were joint together as they spiralled down through the depths, corkscrewing in a slow motioned tailspin on their descent down deeper and deeper.

There did not appear to be an end to their plummet, no floor to thud against heralding the loch bed as they fell, it seemed like a bottomless abyss, unfathomable in measure and measureless in time.

On and on they fell with each holding their eyes tightly closed since the break of the surface ice above them.

The horse still felt his heart beating despite that he was now stalled and no longer galloping.

He had thought earlier that it were compressions of the compaction of his hooves hitting the ground each time shocking his heart to beat but now such movement was over and there it still was, still throbbing in his chest, in fact it was not the jittering thrumming pounding as before, now it was beating normal as if he was relaxed and rested, how could his possibly be?

The anticipation of sharpened daggers from the freezing cold water which he first braced for but strangely the pain never materialised, he never felt cold, or sweaty for that matter.

Just temperate as if back in a long forgotten womb.

The pain, that was previous when topside now seemed away too.

Gently and tentatively the horse opened his mind first to any awaiting prods of agony but none appeared.

He still felt the little girl clamped to his back, her heart beating but slowing to a more acceptable rhythm as his own knock now was.

So with the taction of his precious passenger he knew his senses were not numbed.

But then the biggest shock was yet to be realised...he never felt wet and could breathe as normal, certainly not drowning in a freezing loch.

The severe exhaustion which engulfed the very marrow of his bones and had threaten to stall his continuous flee had now felt abated too, more than just the tiredness diminished, he felt positively energised like never before.

The horse slowly opened his eyes.

He saw darkness around him but lit by a primordial luminesce he could not quite understand, a bioluminescence of no perceived origin.

The sensation of falling down deep in a slow spiral motion continued but not with nauseating speed, it was getting very pleasant actually, with just a slight excited fluttering in his stomach.

It all felt a very strange sensation.

The little girl felt the horse's heart beneath her where she was mounted still on his bare back.

She too was feeling the same sensations as they fell, no pain radiating from her chafed legs anymore, no tiredness.

She gently lifted her head from the horse's neck and opened her eyes to see that same murky illuminated twilight around her with psychedelics blinking in and out of existence and could not comprehend why her lungs were not filling with stagnate salted loch water.

She saw the horse twist his head side to side taking in the coloured sparkles which frizzed and popped around them, some remaining as a gentle glow others darting like fireflies.

'What's happening my beloved" she called into the horse's ear, 'Why are we not dead and drowned?'

I don't understand either my cherished one came a reply within her head as if they were spoken words.

She looked down at the horse knowing this was his worded reply then she said aloud 'you understand what I said!'

I always understood what you said my fond little one.

'But how is this possible my love?' she replied again to the words in her head, 'that I now hear you!'

I am at a lose. The horse spoke to her mind, You hear me too and we talk and you understand my replies.

Some magic has happened for certain. Enchantment or sorcery, the black arts for sure yet I don't feel cursed.

'I am scared dear horse!' cried out the little girl, her voice with a tremble, 'there must be some hex at play here, we are through the ice on the Loch, down into it's depths yet here we breath and talk as if still up above, but sink we do, spinning like a falling sycamore seed in a time slowed down. I fear for us my beloved, I fear!'

'You fear what you don't understand my child' came a gently toned female's voice from the surrounding darkness, unplaceable, neither left, right, up or down.

'Who is that here with us?' shouted out the little girl into the darkness with panic.

Who is doing this taunting? Thought out the horse swiping his head around looking for the source in the darkness.

'Don't fear little one! You that are astride the valiant horse. For I am Mother Earth and you are safe now and sheltered within my arms.'

Gaia? thought out the horse.

'Yes, to some my name is Gaia, to others I am Pachamama or Terra Mater. Some may address me as Kokyangwuti or even Prithvi, it does not matter which as I am simply pure love.'

The surround gloom sparkled different colours as the voice spoke, all tranquil with an opiate like calming effect.

Are we dead? Thought the Stallion out loud, Do you take us down to Tartarus for what was to be my intentions? If so I carry an innocent on my back who should soar but not sink with I. Take this girl from my back into the light I beseech, I will put up no resistance to accept my fate downwards but this little girl does not deserve similar!

'No!' shouting out the girl in response to the horse's statement, 'I go with my beloved horse wherever!' she screamed.

'Fear not. You both are neither dead or alive at this precise moment' the calming voice answered with psychedelic pulsating sparks lightening up around them as if an orchestra was being conducted by the voice.

'Courageous stallion, you face no chastisement as your intents were born from a unadulterated love with a lionhearted braveness of such purity,' the voice continued in answer, 'and sweet girl, your place will always be with your beloved stallion as you are both truly fused by the heart'

The little girl weeped tears of joyful euphoria at this revelation and the horse breathed easier with the great relief from the comforting words delivered.

'But where are we Mother?' the little girl called out to the darkness in a breathless voice 'Where are we going? Where will we end up?'

'You are in my womb my daughter and you will be re-birthed back upon terra-firma soon enough to continue your journey with life.'

The Wolves!, They still wait above with wicked purpose the horse thought out loudly, concern rising again for the little girl.

'The Wolves are neither above or below, and neither are they wicked or righteous,' the voice continued.

'Nature is neither good or bad brave horse, all are my sons and daughters, they act as they do for the clockwork to turn.'

'Does the butterfly not steal the nectar from the flower?' asked the voice 'Does that make him a thief? The bears when he probes into the colony with his sticky tongue to extract the hard working ants, does he become a murder?'

But they would have tortured the my sweet girl! The horse retorted.

'Yes', replied the voice, 'As the cat plays with the mouse and the shark with the seal but do you place such a denomination on them also dear horse?, such being the redness of tooth and claw.'

Then what is the point of Tartarus? Thought the stallion in question, if not for such as the Wolves.

'Tartarus, Orcus, Hell, Inferno, Pandemonium...I know not of such place on my earth' the voice spoke out, 'A scarecrow invented by man to scare some and empower other.

'Tartarus could be the Bastille many may build for themselves during the here and now by using words and actions as if they were the twigs a bird uses to form a nest.

'All living things are architects of their own sufferings or pleasures by the life they choose to led.

'Do you think Fenrir the wolf knows the feeling you have inside when you radiate love on that little girl or how she feels herself when expressing her love onto you?

'That feeling which overflows the heart?

'No, for Fenrir his life is one of wariness and mistrust, looking left then right and behind fearing where and when the next attack to his position will come from.

'No little innocent held his front legs when the she-wolf spewed him out on wet bracken!...He is already living in his own Tartarus never to experience adoration or true devotion only to rule by fear until another comes along and tears out his throat, that is the dangling sword on a thread above his head!'

The horse could understand the rationality in that, not only from the explanation but also the from the feelings which pulses around him as if parting awareness onto his consciousness too.

He shared a blessed existence with the little girl always close by, he would never exchange such memories for anything.

'What will happen now Mother?' the little girl piped up.

'Now you both return and carry on with your existence. Then you must love my child, you must love because love is what is important, without love there is nothing.

'Love is how you must leave your mark on this world and such devotion that you give will be the legacy you leave behind and that, my sweet girl, is how you and brave horse will be remembered and the tale of which will be told then retold again down the ages!'

'Valient horse would gladly sacrifice himself on the altar of love to save you and I see you would do the same for him such is this love you both share,' continued the voice.

'Other love will also be found as directed by my brother Eros as we are both begotten by the primordial Chaos down the Hesiodic chain.

But have patience sweet soul for in your story I know the turns it will take.

'And it shall be that true love which awakes you my dear little girl, and always remember that during the course of love there may be bumps and hurdles then also remember such was your journey from village to the Haven but through love you got there in the end!'

'Now is the time to return to the world you know, live your life again and remember these lessons'

The voice seemed to get distant as she finished and as the air got heavier, the pair got drowsier.

They continued to float gently downwards like a feather from a nest up high.

Continuing to spiral around slowly but then their circling started to drawn in and gather momentum, faster and faster.

The little girl held the horse's mane tightly. She lowered her head and closed her eyes as the stallion closed his too.

They spun with increasing velocity until they both gradually passed out in a deep hypnotic sleep as if induced by the poppy.

Back on the salt plains the wolf pack trudged home, exhausted and with empty bellies.

It would be a long walk back to the grasslands.

Fenrir was in front, as Alpha he led the pack.

He was still frothing with so much fury that he never realised when the other two wolves creep up, one on each side of him just outside of his periphery view.

His rage had subdued his senses.

He heard a low growl to his left and turned his head in that direction, it was the same challenger as before, the one who raced up to his side during the chase.

He twisted his head around some more then snarled corrugating his muzzle and displaying his fangs.

Suddenly a jaw clamped on the top his neck from the opposite side and then he felt claws pierce into his rump from the rear weight him downwards.

He raised his head up in attempt to throw off the moored jaws from above, this upwards thrust exposed his throat from beneath which was then raggedly ripped out by a force at his left from the first wolf which had first drawn his attention.

He was set upon by three of the pack, a coordinated attack to which his struggled defence was to be futile against.

His last thoughts as his windpipe was torn out from his neck was pure loathing and hatred then not another thought was to be had as his dead body was ragged across the salty ground by the rest of the pack only leaving read smears to paint where his existence had came to an end.

It was a beautiful sunny morning, not a cloud in the sky as the young man walked from the Haven's village huts across to the fruit trees to pick some pomegranates to take back to have later with his mother for lunch.

The dawn dew still left its trace on the grass as he walked across to the trees dampening his ankles just above the throat of his moccasins.

Looking across he saw what he thought to be someone slumbering at the foot of the tree.

He wondered why someone would choose to have a nap under that big tree at such an early time in the morning, or, he thought to himself, perhaps the person had slept there all night.

At first from the distance and angle of his approach it appeared that the sleeping form was resting on the top of some smooth filled brown hessian sacks.

But upon arriving closer he could see they were not sacks at all but actually a very healthy and strong looking stallion in his prime which was also lying slightly curled asleep, platforming the figure up off from the morning's dampness which was on the ground.

The figure which he could now identify as a beautiful lithe young woman, similar age to himself, who was silent in a sleeping slumber laying on the horse's back, her legs over it's haunches luxuriating with the radiating equine body heat.

She wore only a simple spun white cotton dress down to just below her knees, immaculate with not a mark on it, as clean as a baby's conscience, as was the horse too.

The horse was exquisitely groomed with the black keratin of his hooves without the slightest scrape on them, its chestnut hide brushed to a sheen.

The young woman's long black hair fanned out over the horses mane. Both hair and mane intertwined each other where they lay together, chestnut brown merged with midnight black and dappled with blooms of red flowers.

The red begonias had been meticulously woven into both the woman's hair and the horse's mane.

Her arms were stretched slightly out to the front of her sleeping form holding a small posey of these same flowers which were in her hair as if she was walking up an aisle to get wed.

On the inside of her left forearm was the tattooed outline of a galloping horse.

Both horse and young woman slept soundly as if exhausted.

Delicately the woman's body would raise up slightly with each breath the sleeping horse silently inhaled then lowered back done with the exhale as she was afloat on a calm sea.

The boy stood and starred, entranced by her beauty, completely bewitched.

He felt a quickening of his heart and a shortness of his breath at the sight presented in front of him.

Now there lay a woman worthy of love he thought, and a horse to be prized and taken care of.

GOLDBAR & DOUGAL

Stories often start with a Once Upon a Time. Our tale here also does as it took place once upon a time, during a period in the past, a time almost forgotten to this here old grandnannie of yours.

It would be a time when your grandbubbie was still alive and he and I would gallop the fields together.

The story I am about to tell you is a true one, as true as the summer days are long.

I will try to recall the details of this old yarn as I once told it to your popsicle when he was a similar age to you before he met up with your momsicle.

Now be patient with this here old straw chewer.

I am long in tooth and patchy of hide so dredging up this old record of the past will take some concentration on my part but I will get there.

A story carried down the generations is like a piece of tree bark floating down a brook, similar to that one across there yonder at the end of these meadows, that slip of a stream you so do enjoy dipping your hoofs into after a day's frolicking in the pastures.

This piece of bark, which like a story through the years, floats downstream bouncing as if a pinball affa every nugget of half submerged boulder with which it meets along its journey.

Upon bumping into these new acquaintances it leaves a few freckles behind.

As I tell you this here tale there's maybe a few splinters of details that I have forget from when my own sires first told me many years when I was your age, as they in turn would have forgotten since when their begetters had told them.

I dare say when the day cometh for you to tell it to your future little one even some more freckles will have been fallen affa it too.

Eventually one day this here drifting bark of a tale which I am about to tell you will just be the size of a pine needle floating along then a hungry trout will mistake it for a tiny bite sized beastie and gobble it whole, then it will be no more, maybe just an ache in a fish's belly.

Tis' a tale of a deuce of horses. I see with the your tilt and pawing of them there dandelion stubs you don't know what the meaning of a deuce is so I'll tell you. It mean a pair, a twain of the same and those two gee-gee were the same as in a compatible set.

But they also had their differences too let us not forget that, and I don't just mean their upbringing or breed.

One was a mighty Clydesdale, wide in the shoulders with hooves the size of dinner plates.

This big stallion's name was Dougal. Aye, as Scottish as the heathers as he was raised from a breed which once pulled the barges along the River Clyde on the side which the sun sets far away in a land called Scotland.

A draught horse they'd called his type, good for drawing heavy loads and herculean strong I tell you, faithful and hard working to the very last.

Twenty-two hand spans from hoof to crest, and no wee little maiden's hands let it be known, these would be the open colossal mitts of a smithy with sooty paws big enough to hoist an anvil above his head with the one claw.

He was gingery cinnamon, the colour of an autumn sunset with a white stripe down his muzzle. He also had an abundance of scars which striped his hindquarters and back to remind him that not every horse owner is a kindly one.

Then there was his mare, a beautiful palomino lusitano shaded the hue of the gilt encased on a Monarch butterfly's wings such was the velvet of her hide which would shimmer as if gold when the light bounced off of her.

She were dainty with an elegant long blond mane.

Warm blooded and intelligent as they come with a nimble trot and a lightening gallop. Her name was, wait, let me think.

Trying to recall here, the auld grey matter up here in my noggin is not what it once was.

As I said, freckles dropping off and all that...but I remember now. Ah yes of course, she was called Goldbar on account of her long flanks which would look like gold in the glint and glimmer of the sun.

Well Goldbar and Dougal looked an odd pair together side by side right enough.

The muckle great big Dougal was a clumsy brute. He was ponderous and slow in his actions.

He would look down at the grass with every tread, his head bowed low as if he had no confidence, whereas Goodbar was graceful as a wood fairy, she'd hold her head up proudly looking at the sun and watching the whispery clouds sail across the sky.

Goldbar was impulsive to act, Dougal was cautious. Green light and red light, one go, one stop but even coins need two sides like a Ying and a Yang.

What's a Ying and Yang you ask? Well it's a mixing of the two energies that's makes life possible but the balance needs to always be in check. Not too much Ying without enough Yang, and the same is with horses too as it is with people.

I'd already told you they were a deuce and never a truer word spoken. Now maybe not to the gander as they did look an peculiar matched pair but in their spirit they were the perfect fit together as they profoundly complimented one other, and where else does it really matter but in the heart.

There was never a truer love than what was shared between these two horses.

As we age our teeth grow longer, we get grey around the muzzle and our lips droop like a water ladened leaf, but our essence never changes and that's where we really need to find a match when we look for our soul mate.

We need someone that reaches and entwines with our spirit. I use the example of what I found once in my life with your old grandbubbie, although he passed before your time so you never got to meet him, such a tragedy which that is.

Anyway, that's what we really need in life, a true mate! So dial back your heat young one when you look across at these fillies in the meadows next door.

Be patient and when the right one appears you will just know, she will take your breath away and command your every thought day and night, but I get off track, the old romantic in me always looks for dominance , back to preparing our tale at hand.

Later in the evenings when the sun in the sky would dip, then the moon would rise and take up her post in its place, Goldbar would rest her muzzle across Dougal's dunked curtsied neck as they stood together under the mango tree in their field.

He would feel her warmth latch across the top of his scruff then settle his peace with the day which had passed to then go meet his dreams and again always with his Goldbar in them.

During the day when Dougal was in from working the fields he would stand at the sideline and watch Goldbar frolicking around the acreage of the pastures whilst he kept his eyes open scanning for chuckholes and slithering asps which could be in her path.

He was her protector and as such he stood guard.

Goldbar would snort across at him, run towards then dash onwards wanting Dougal to come join her.

Why look so serious? Come and enjoy yourself, her look would present but Dougal's pleasure was to behold her vivacity of life and to be there should she need him.

He would be her anchor if she were ever to drift into dangerous oceans, that was his contentment, his state of happiness, a gratification he once would have never believed possible. To feel such love and so readily commit absolutely to it.

Goldbar would nuzzle into Dougal when he was moody and sullen if after a frustrating day of dragging the plough across one of the rocky fields and believe me, he could be a stubborn grumpy big shire at times, a previous life had dealt him no favours.

Sometimes he would return to the pastures with a feeling of dragons in his fuzzgutton but Goldbar would turn these tension hydras into butterflies which would flip flap away.

You see, Goldbar was something of a healer, she knew how to make pain go away like the mists of a morning when day starts to mature.

A healer she was I tell you, just like your old gran here when you gobble up a mouthful of thistles by mistake! Then I treat you with the milk of dandelion to sooth your ills.

Well Goldbar's healing was not such of the organic alchemy type, but was more of the spiritual kind and she would delivered her medicine through her love and tenderness.

They were in love like swans on a lake and the dew upon the grass. The daisies would grow abundantly in the field under their hoofs as the sun would heat the soil and all was good in the world.

So snuggle in and get all comfy my little one. Lets start this tale with a Once Upon a Time as the tradition of story telling demands …

…in a place faraway there was a farm.

It was a happy farm with an abundance of joy, the animals were content and well cared for.

The cows in the field were chilled out contently watching the passing of the day whilst chewing the cud.

The chickens would scurry and scratch at the dirt energetically zigzagging with joyful craziness.

The Farmer was a jolly man with an easy going temperament and always wearing a big smile. His name was Eamon.

He was a content man who worked very hard for the life which he had and enjoyed his comforts at the end of the day.

Not being a slave to fashion and preferring comfort over appearing dapper, his usual attired was an old brown pair of corduroy trousers with patches over the knees and a white shirt with short sleeves, usually the first clean one within his reach on the mornings which he'd normally find draped over the chair as laid there the night before by his wife for him to wear as not to simply use the same one from the other day.

His only jewellery was the wide gold wedding ring he wore with pride and a loose fitting watch with a silver bracelet which would slip more up his arm than lay on his wrist.

The only different outfit you would see him wear would be an old pair of blue dungarees which he would put on whilst working on the farm which was most days from sunrise until sunset.

He loved his wife and little girl, and would often sit out on his porch with them after dinner watching the crepusular light of the sun setting whilst his daughter drew on paper with her crayons and his wife would read a book using the last of the day's light.

He especially liked sitting out there comfortable on his wicker chair.

He felt there could be no more in this world that the satisfaction of being in the company of his much loved little family whilst watching the slanting last rays of the setting sun gave a warm rose tinge to the sky as it retreated for the evening dipping down under the horizon of his own land which he had toiled so hard working upon such was his simple pleasures in life, perhaps that and the one jar of hoppy beer he would allow himself during such moments.

It was a small kingdom he surveyed and his subject were not many but he considered life to be so very good.

Farmer Eamon's wife, whose name was Sileas, was a painter, an artist.

During the day, when she was not giving lessons to their daughter or preparing lunch and dinner for the small family, she would plant her easel just outside the farm house where she would sit on a chair and stain the canvas with various watercolours reproducing the generous enchantment that was within her vision.

She considered herself spoilt with the natural beauty of where they lived at the farm, and the generosity of the sights around her would deliver much to allow Sileas to traverse around her paint palette with her brush as the record on the canvases she produced would testify to.

Sileas and Eamon's daughter was called Bell.

She was aged six and quite bijou in statue for her age.

Bell was homeschooled by her mother but she did attend some classes in village hall once or twice a week as her parents also wanted her not to miss out on the social development with her peers as more of an isolated existence on the farm could otherwise be to her detriment regarding her social skills with others outside of their small family.

Sileas would take Bell to the village during these morning on the little buggy pulled by Goldbar.

After dropping Bell off at the hall Sileas herself would continue into the small village to collect some groceries after which she would then tether Goldbar to the beam in the shade of the barn with some fresh water.

The Sileas would visit the little cooperation tea room to catch up on the gossip and perhaps leave one of her newly completed painting there where it would be put on the wall and labelled for sale, a few extra bucks for the family to supplement their income which was mostly from the produce they grew on the farm.

When at home and not taking lessons or doing chores Bell would run around the farm chase after the chickens or feed the cows hand picked wads of grass from the fence.

But her most favourite time would be when she'd braid and tie pretty blue ribbons onto Goldbar's blonde flowing mane.

This would be mostly later on in the afternoons when the elegant Goldbar shared the field with her cumbersome partner Dougal as the pair were inseparable once the big Clydesdale horse had finished his work for the day with Bell's father Eamon.

They looked the odd couple to Bell's eyes, as they did to everyone eyes as it was said.

Goldbar with her polished elegance, then there was Dougal with his brute build and scars but, as Sileas would tell to her daughter that with everything in life looks can be deceiving and we should not judge on what our eyes take in as they make a unreliable witness to the reality and this was certainly so very true with these two horses, you could tell from a mile that they were very much in love.

Dougal was a gentle stallion, he was quiet and tender especially around Goldbar and Bell.

Sileas and Eamon would never have any concerns when his daughter Bell was in the field standing on her little green upturned Antartica crate braiding Goldbar's mane then Dougal too would stand there watching, looking almost entertained at the spectacle of petit Bell standing on her box tangling Goldbar's locks and weaving in the ribbons.

Goldbar would stand there with neither a nudge or a nay as Bell worked away with her minuscule junior fingers on her mane.

Once she was finished and down from her crated platform Dougal would come closer as if to inspect her work on his love then would give out a snort as if expressing his approval.

Sileas had umpteen paintings and sketches of Bell standing there, her small statue perched on the green crate reaching up lacing the braids with the two powerful equine figures peacefully beside her.

When Eamon first bought Dougal at the auction he was very wary about putting this big mistreated older Clydesdale in the same paddock as his beloved mare but after while, and with much oats and tentative attention, he could see a great gentleness in the scarred horse he never expected from such a massive stallion with a history of being abused by it's previous owner.

Before placing them together Eamon was to watch Goldbar, who he also considered a good judge of character.

She appeared to take an interest in the big horse as they were always standing close together separated only by the fence, heads close together to each other, eyes half closed as if Goldbar was healing the big stallion with her love.

The farmer decided to give Dougal the chance and opened the gate to his paddock to allow him to enter into Goldbar's field whilst he stood watching, ready to intervene at the slightest sign of trouble.

Strangely Dougal stood frozen once the connecting gate was opened.

He looked at the farmer as if to ask permission as to if it would be ok to proceed through the opening.

Eamon nodded his consent but the big horse continued just to stand there until the farmer came across to him then gently walked him through the open gate.

Eamon then stood back and watch cautiously as Dougal strode up toward Goldbar.

Once together they started to groom each other immediately as if they'd been partners for years.

Eamon was truly amazed! Such was the power of love he'd thought to himself.

Over the coming weeks the two horses only seemed to bond more and more. They would canter around the field at a happy gait with their flanks almost touching each others.

Eamon was so glad to see his bar of gold so happy, and to see the once abused stallion recovered in such a miraculous way.

He would tell his wife as they sat out on the porch looking across at the stallion and mare standing under the tree across in the field during the evenings, 'I do believe we are witnesses to a true love here my dear darling. I think a certain two horses have found love under the mango tree.'

Sileas would giggle and add 'I always knew our Goldbar was a healer, proof of equine therapy right there without question.'

They'd both laughed at this then continue to watch the sun set looking across at the two lovers under the mango tree.

Farmer Eamon knew some of Dougal's history.

He knew of the big Clydesdale's previous owner, a farmer by the name Arthur Ludd.

Ludd had a deserved reputation of being a violent drunk who'd often frequent the tavern in the village and let his fists do the talking if he'd heard anything to which he would disagree with.

He was certainly not the type of acquaintance Eamon would share or even give the time of the day to, nor was the Black Dog Tavern the sort of place he would ever consider visiting.

Eamon heard the stories about Ludd from the other farmers in the village. They'd mention how he would arrive to the tavern on the back of the big Clydesdale horse, then leave him tied up outside with a short rope attached to a tight halter for hours on end in all types of weather without water.

Then when he crawled or was thrown out the tavern by closing time he would be so drunk he could not get upon his horse so would kick and whip it as if the stallion was to blame before walking stinkingly intoxicated home whilst still leaving the horse tied up there overnight beaten and blooded without food or water.

Eamon never even really knew the worst, he could only guess from the marking on Dougal's hide as to what tortures the horse had to endure during his years with the cruel Ludd. It stung Eamon's heart that such a gentle animal had suffered so much.

The details which thankfully Eamon never got to know were that Farmer Lund would work Dougal to exhaustion then would whip and kick him at the slightest whim.

Dougal would never retaliate, as a strapping enormous Clydesdale he could have kicked Ludd into the middle of the next week, but Dougal would never hurt a fly and Farmer Ludd, like all cowards, knew this to his own advantage and did not spare the rod.

Ludd would scream and shout at the horse too…'You big ugly brute, pull harder…faster…an fat old donkey could do better!', 'never a lazier clod have I ever seen, ma auld ma could pull harder than you ya lazy good for nothing lump!'

He'd use Dougal to plough the earth in the fence enclosed paddocks of his farm. The blade on the plough was blunt from Ludd's laziness to sharpen it and needed such effort from Dougal to score it across the hardened earth that it strained every equine sinew and tendon within his body.

The unkept field of thorns and brambles torn into the soft parts of Dougal's legs too and his hooves ached as they were untrimmed because Ludd would not pay money for a farrier to do the work, instead he would attempt the job himself with unskilled butchery after a bucket of his gutrot home brew which he would drink after getting barred from the tavern in the village, something which just made his temper worse.

At first Dougal would desperately try to avoid the whips and kicks that Ludd would dish out.

He would attempt to circle the paddock to stay out of Ludd's range hoping that he'd exhausted himself, that his rage would subdue somewhat, but Ludd could always corner the horse, and god forbid if Dougal tried to leave the paddock through the opening in the fence as then Ludd would dish out a punishment much worst as he'd would normally do.

If Dougal tried to leave, Ludd would attach a rope halter around the horse's thick neck pulling his head down low then scourge his back with the crop before leaving him overnight in that position.

Dougal soon associated attempting to leave the paddock without being led out would result is a terrible unbearable brutal torture.

Not long after he would just stand there and take the beatings as being the least of a dragged out suffering.

Such terrible events left not only the physical scars which were so clearly visible on his hide but also deep psychological damage too.

To that day Dougal would always need to seek permission from his new master before leaving one field into another or be led through a gate.

Eamon, who was a polar opposite to the cruel Ludd never understood the reasons why, he'd thought this was an obedience of Dougal, the horse's amenable mannerism.

He never got to know just how deeply Dougal's damage ran within the horse's subconscious.

Eventually Farmer Ludd's drinking habits forced him to sell his farm and that was when Eamon first saw Dougal when he attended the auction.

The horse looked a shadow of himself then compared to how he was to look later.

He was haggard looking at the auction, extremely thin and malnourished with a dejected posture.

The other bidders in attendance thought the threadbare scabby horse was only fit for the glue factory but thankfully the kindly Eamon took pity and purchased Dougal bringing him back to his farm where there he would nurse him back to health with buckets of oats and a gentleness of touch.

Goldbar did not know the extent of Dougal's suffering at the hand's of his previous owner. She'd knew he had been through much, the marking on his skin certainly illustrated that sorry tale and also how he looked when he first arrived on the farm.

She would never forget how despondent his eyes looked.

He was terribly thin and covered in untreated sores.

She could remember Eamon had got the vet to come out and look him over.

He was given supplements and put on a special diet which contained lots of alfalfa and special grains. Ointment was applied to the oozing blisters on his flesh.

Although he had started putting on weight again still she sensed something much deeper which was crushing his spirit, she soon was to understand that it this was his lack of self-worth, he was just existing but not truly living.

There were other time also when she could sense darker moments arriving within Dougal, when depression would ascend upon him.

His dark memories which would then arise without warrant casting their stygian murky undertakings to eclipse his mind and obscure the delight he'd since found in later life on the farm with Goldbar.

These inner dragons would attempt to grapple into his heart with their serpent like talons as to get a deeper hold onto him.

Goldbar recognising his inner turmoil so would be there to chase these black shadows back as not to defile Dougal's new growing feeling of worth.

She would drive them off with her caresses.

Transform their clawing into a gentler flutter of a butterfly's wings with her touch, only then to be brush away, casted off like pollen from a flower as she lead Dougal back into to light.

Goldbar did not fully understand the cause of the bleakness which would sometimes arrive in her mate.

They were not as frequent as they once were when he first arrived on the farm. She did not know the history of his previous life in much details but she could see from the deep scars which crisscrossed his rears and draped across his back that it had not been a good epoch for him.

She'd never knew such suffering herself having been born on the very farm which she now shared with Dougal.

The farmer there, with his family, were always so loving and kind with her. Although she did realise that out there beyond their farm's boundaries it was not all like what she had there.

She'd often see other visiting farmers who would come to deliver with their carts. Some of these visiting horse had such despondency in their eyes. Almost a similar sadness to which she'd saw glazing Dougal's during his moments of darkness, yet never quite as intense.

She'd flinch upon hearing the crack of the whip as a cart was driven off after dropping their delivered sacks of corn and oats had been deposited.

Eamon would sense her fear then and comfort her with soft words whilst scowling a frown at the departing riders.

'Don't you fear my love,' he would say, 'no whip, birch or spur will ever touch the skin of any of my animals here.'

During the days, early in the mornings, after they had a good fill of oats, Dougal would tenderly, with his nose to her neck, kiss Goldbar a goodbye as Farmer Eamon would come and collect him and walk him through the gate then across to one of the fields to do some ploughing.

On this, which was such a fresh morning it were to be in what they called Stoney Paddock.

It was named such due to the plethora quantity of rocks scattered around the field.

This was going to be a hard day and Dougal had taken an extra pull on the oats that morning for more energy in preparation for the day ahead.

Luckily Eamon was a kindly farmer who when behind the plough would not push his steed hard so Dougal was not overly concerned at the task waiting them.

Eamon fitted Dougal with the bridle and harness, 'not too tight old friend?' he would ask with concern as was his custom during these moments to which Dougal would snort and move his head as if in intelligent response, but of course, there could be no easy communication between the pair.

Eamon's words would be like a foreign language to the equine auricles but Dougal's ears always stood at attention with the respect he had for this old farmer who he loved like a father, and he could tell from the tones that it was only affection spoken to him.

It had to be said that Goldbar was much closer to Eamon than Dougal could be as she was there with the farmer from her very beginnings as she was foaled on the farm with Eamon's aid.

There was a connection between the two which any new comer such as Dougal could never reach.

The tenderness Goldbar felt towards the old farmer was almost akin to father and daughter if that could be said about a horse and a human.

She appeared to comprehend every word that he spoke to her.

When not being adorned with braids and ribbons by the young Bell, Goldbar's only other role on the farm was, as mentioned previously, to pull the buggy with Sileas and Bell sitting high upon it's wooden bench to take them to the village.

It was usually twice a week and today would be that day again.

They did own one of these new fangled petrol fuelled jalopies which Eamon liked to keep ticking over and tinkering with in the barn, but the old ways were still one of the preferred eccentricities of the local area and oats were cheaper than oil with the byproduct feeding the roses.

Goldbar looked forward to these moments with great excitement. She loved pulling the little bright yellow carriage along the farm lane toward the market.

She would trot along with such gaiety and cheer looking forward to seeing Dougal again once she'd return as it usually timed with him finishing his labours for the day so then they could relax together standing under the old mango tree near the fence.

* * *

Her favourite part of these twice a week excursions was the preparation done on her by the old farmer who would come across and fitting her with the driving harness, a comfortable leather decorated with painted daisies as was Bell's fun.

Farmer Eamon came across now, taking a well earned break from the ploughing with her beloved Dougal who was still in Stoney Paddock munching down on some oats he'd been given, a deserved midmorning treat.

'How are you today Goldbar my love?' Eamon asked standing around by her face rubbing her nose affectionately.

She understood every word and snuggled her face into his shoulder with much love and regard.

He looked worn and exhausted she's thought, she would tell Dougal later to slow down the ploughing, Eamon was not getting any younger and should take it easy, especially working in that accursed Stoney Paddock, it would be a hard graft even for a younger man as it was really tough going, as Dougal's muscles will testify tonight she thought.

'I love you my dear,' the farmer continued, 'you look after my Sileas and little Bell this morning when taking them to village. Watch out for the other buggies at the junction up top of lane! These two Ladies that you will be carrying are precious cargo, just like you are my bar of gold.' Then he gave Goldbar a kiss on her nose as was his custom.

Goldbar closed her long lashed eyes at the pleasure of the attention she received, how she loved this old kindly man. He was the most benevolent soul to her ever since she was a foal stumbling on shaky amniotic soaked legs in the field after she was born, the affection and devotion she felt towards this man knew no boundaries.

As he chewed on the oats which the old farmer had left him before he had went up ahead to harness his beloved Goldbar for the ladies to visit the market Dougal looked across at his dear love getting prepared for the day's outing.

What a feeling of happiness surrounded him. This was what pure happiness felt like he thought to himself, the contentment of giving out love and feeling it received in return.

It had been a hard early mornings so far ploughing in the field, the sun had baked the earth hard and these stones seemed to be getting increasingly bounteous on every rotation when they worked this ground.

The rocks seem to be growing in more abundance than the potatoes which they had planned to plant later.

Dougal had worked up quite a sheen on his coat, he will need a good hose down before Goldbar returns later, she liked her stallion fresh and clean.

The old farmer this morning seemed to have been building up quite a sweat too the horse thought.

When he would come around Dougal's flank he could see the steam raise from his perspiration that morning.

Dougal had slowed his pace hoping old Eamon would take it a bit easier, something Dougal would never have dared to even contemplate with his previous owner Farmer Ludd or he would have felt the sting of the whip or whirl of the coup. Thank goodness Eamon was nothing like the previous farmer he worked for.

Eamon was most compassionate person ever, even just that very morning he had stuck a couple of big rosey apples in Dougal's oats to compliment his feed, Dougal loved the farmer and treasured their time together working the fields, even when the work as as tough as it was proving to be on that day.

Goldbar with harness fitted and buggy attached, set off at a quick trot toward the village with her adored load of Sileas and Bell behind her on the buggy's bench.

Eamon stood there waving his three ladies off wishing them a fair and pleasant trip.

He removed his hanky from the top pocket of his shirt and whipped his brow, he was feeling it today, he should really think about taking it more easy at his age, perhaps buy one of these new fancy sounding tractors which he has been hearing about, this would also give Dougal some more time with Goldbar he thought to himself.

But he so enjoyed getting his hands on the harness straps too much, he could never imagine his nails without the dirt of his land under them, and there was a certain tranquillity working his own fields with Dougal, he enjoyed these moments so very much even when labouring on that damned hard patch in Stoney Paddock.

Off he marched to get back to work with Dougal, the quicker they were to resume the sooner they would be finish and Eamon wanted to be changed, scrubbed and waiting for his family's return so he could sit and hear all about their day.

Dougal saw the farmer approaching and let out a snort of rapture relishing some more work with the farmer, his heart was still pumped and beating fast after seeing his beloved Goldbar amble off up the lane.

As Eamon walked across to Dougal, who had been untethered from the plough to enjoy his lunch within the paddock, he saw a large rock sticking out from part of the unploughed earth.

Best toss that aside before it could blunt the ploughshare blade if it were to goes over it, he thought to himself as he bent down to tug it from the hard compressed soil, but then as he bend he felt an intense flaring pain shoot up his left arm.

Whilst trying to righten himself back up from his bend position he then fell to the ground with a shortening of breath.

It was like a cramp down his left side which then spread across his upper body like a steel band tightening.

Eamon grasped his right hand across his chest to hold his left arm lying there on the ground as he scrunched up his face to the heavens in pain.

Dougal witnessed the farmer bend to pick up what he thought must be a rock then fall to the ground.

His first thought was that Eamon had simple unbalanced and fallen over but then he could then see, even from the distance, the look on the farmer's face.

Dougal snorted loudly and raced toward the prone Eamon who now lay still on the cold hard earth as his movements had ceased.

When Dougal reached him he pressed his face down toward Eamon's and snorted, he stamped the earth with his hoof making the ground vibrate trying to get a reaction from the prostrate man but nothing, no response was forthcoming from the felled farmer.

The big horse could not understand what had happened but knew this was very wrong! This was bad, definitely bad!

He thudded the ground more with his hoofs then started galloping heavily around the paddock field whining and neighing loudly with a panic building in his great chest.

He looked across to the farm house for help but they had already left with Goldbar towing the buggy to the market.

Dougal rearer up and dropped his heavy front quarters to the compacted dirt again and again repeatedly.

What is to be done? he demanded of himself frustrated that an answer could not be found.

He ran to where the farmer lay again and pulled at his leg on the ground pawing with his hoof, nothing...no reaction except the momentum Dougal himself had stirred.

Eamon was dead!

Dougal never knew the concept of death and was confused, he just knew something was terribly wrong so he ran around the field left then right, snorting and neighing, he was distressed and in hysteric frenzy of worry.

Dougal wanted to race out through paddock gate to seek help but a Pavlovian conditioning from his past traumas caused by the callous Farmer Ludd prevented him to do so.

Flashbacks of the tightening rope halter pulling him down to his hocks then the flaying of his skin projected across his mind like a nightmarish strobe.

He flinch physically with the mental recalling of the agony of the whip against his hide.

His submerged mind controlled him like an invisible jockey on his back, he just could not leave through the gate! He was a captive in the paddock despite the opening being unbarred and agape.

Whereas intuition can teach that it's not necessary to have had experienced of a burn to fear the fire or to have nearly drowned to dread the water, some traumas can be so convincingly powerful that it can easily be mistaken for intuition by part of the subconsciousness to feel such a terror towards an element or reason which had led up to such distress!

Dougal, despite his lathered hysteria driven desperation, could not force himself out from the confines of the fenced paddock through the presented opened gate.

It was to be another six hours before Goldbar returned hauling the buggy behind her.

Immediately she could sense something was very wrong when she saw Dougal hither and thither across within Stoney Paddock.

With great unease Sileas sensed it too.

'Wait with in the buggy with Goldbar!' Sileas shouted at Bell whilst stepping down from the carriage then running across to the paddock.

She saw her husband lying there instantly and at first she told her racing mind that surely he has fallen, perhaps bumped his head on one of the many rocks, yet the reality kept echoing back to her that this situation was far more severe and as she approached closer she started to realise it could not get more dire than this!

'Wow, wow!' she screamed at Dougal who was still in a near frenzy.

She bend down to comfort Eamon but could see his lips were already blue and there was no animation in his pale now stiffened face.

'Mama Mama, what's happened?' She heard the little voice by her side and realised just then that Bell had ran after her when she jumped down out of the buggy and sprinted towards the paddock.

Still on her knees she twisted around then reached across to her Bell and hugged her tightly, blinkering the girl's sight away from her deceased father muffing both sobs and tears into the small furry collar of her jacket.

Goldbar could only stand and watched from the fence of the paddock, unable to get closer as still attached to the buggy with its axle too wide to enter through the opening.

Dougal, now slightly more calm walked slowly across to the side of the fence and looked across at the mare desperately needing her touch of reassurance and also wanting to comfort her.

Goldbar looked across at him but did not approach any closer, she could not understand what she was witnessing when we saw Sileas holding Bell as they cried beside the fallen unmoving figure of Eamon but realised something really terrible had happened and life would never be the same.

So also started to wonder why Dougal would not leave the paddock and come to her in this, which was her time of need.

He should come out of the enclosure to be with her there close beside her and nuzzle her in her state of sadness and confusion!

She needed this from his now!

He was supposed to be her protector, she needed his care and protection that very moment, where is the stallion she supported at his worst moments of his rehabilitation to reciprocate her love now during this time and what was becoming the unfolding of what would be the wave of a great sadness that see can see coming to engulf her?

Why did he not come out of the field to care instead of standing there on the other side of the fence just looking across at her.

It had been two weeks since Farmer Eamon's funeral and the farm was in mourning, even the most excitable chickens seemed subdued and the cows chewed the curd with less vigour.

Stoney Paddock remained only half ploughed as the contrasting two toned earth would testify, almost like a memorial to the departed ploughman.

Sileas sat on the porch most of these days just looking out across the fields in silence. Bella was quiet too following her mother's led. Only the smallest of talk was exchanged between mother and daughter.

In the field Goldbar would stand alone under the mango tree with her head lowered, her back drooped and empty eyes staring out but not seeing.

The braids that were once in her mane with the blue ribbons were no longer there.

Dougal stood further along in the field away from Goldbar.

Since the farmer's tragic death he'd felt a change in his beloved mare, he sensed the love she once had for him was no longer there yet his affection for her were still a constant and never missed a beat.

If he were to approach her where she stood under the mango tree she would just then move off out from under its shade then further out into the field as to get away from him.

Then if he were to follow, she would just move on again repeating the movement to keep the distance between them. His heart was broken seeing her do this. She would not allow him close.

Dougal would walk across to where the carambola tree extended the reach of its branches across the fence and gently pick up wind fallen fruit in his mouth. Then he would walk it over to where Goldbar grieved under the mango tree, just before reaching the threshold, an unmarked boarder which if crossed would elicit her flitting away from him again. There he would then drop the fruit and back away as if surrendering.

Soon there was to be a small pile of untouched transported carambolas staring up at him from out of the grass where he had made the previous deposits as he added another one to the growing mound of unwanted offerings.

Goldbar was not eating, even the oats went barely touched by her yet this was not her purpose as why she refuse the gifts from the stallion, he knew it was a case of her not wanting to acknowledge him in the least way such was the profound rejection that she would give him.

Dougal could see the darkness of depression that shrouded the love of his life, he knew the shadows well from his own experiences but did not know how to help his love if she would not let him close and wanted nothing to do with him.

He felt enfeebled and inadequate to comfort the mare he so very much loved.

It was a profound impotence, a frustration that led him to do wrong when he tried so hard only to do right by her.

He should have gave her space allowing her to come to terms with the maelstrom of emotions which were coursing through her but it felt counter to his instincts as to stay away from the one he loved so very much. With every ounce of his being he could not stand it.

Yet when some part of him realised that this was what was needed, then the other part disagreed and demanded he should act before it were too late!

His emotions would go ups and down like beam above the blade of the plough would do when he and the farmer worked Molehill paddock in the past, a memory of which now stung his heart as this would never be again since the farmer was no longer there.

He was experiencing hundreds emotions within minutes oscillating through his head. The feeling of each was an act without an interval upon his confused brain.

He would feel his heart pound with hope when he would approach her at the mango tree, a feeling fuelled with the need to actually being doing something more than simply waiting, but then when she'd lift up hoofs and move away his heart would beat even more with the disappointment, harden it would sink even deeper within this chest.

He wished he could have done more, both in that damned Stoney Paddock when the farmer fell but also after the buggy arrived back and he saw Goldbar on the the other side of the fence, his love, his soul mate.

He wished so very hard that he could have vaulted the fence like a Hanoverian, but he was a heavy drey horse thick of tough muscle and sinew, he was not such an equestrian.

The most obvious exit then to have used as to reach then comfort his love would of course have been the paddock entrance opening, but alone he just could not leave that field due to the demons of his past hauling him back like a puppeteer with a rebellious marionette and as such he had failed his love Goldbar.

All attempts to ameliorate himself over this went poorly.

Goldbar who once gazed up to the skies now starred at the ground, the infinity of the heavens traded for the single dimension of the earth such was her emotional state.

She looked at the accumulating pile of carambolas on the ground just out the shade of the mango tree.

Black ants now marched over the surfaces of the angled yellow pods, soldiers in the action of decay just following the commands of nature.

She felt betrayed and letdown by the very horse she had expected to be there for her at her worst moment.

She could also see him suffering and felt pity but just could not let him get close to her. There now was an emptiness in her which was once filled with love.

The azure that was their horizon together now seemed bleak and cloudy, the dreams they shared since swept away in the storm.

She could not see a future with his clumsy stallion who she once found so gentle and loving.

Here he came again she noticed without making eye contact, another carambola wedged in that mouth to add to the decaying pile, food for the ants, the pity she shortly before felt then turning to a disgust for that moment. With his gestures now she only felt a bitterness within her as a witness to the display, anything he was to do felt to her as a pathetic act.

Why can't he just leave me to regain my balance she thought, every time he drops one of these damned fruits there I only feel an anger which then turns to a pity later as I don't want him suffering.

I did once have love for this lump but then when I see him my resent comes flooding back with an overriding fury and soon I feel confused such is the rollercoaster ride of emotions.

Again Dougal repeated the process.

As he dropped the fruit he would feel a brief loosening of the tension within in his heart which occurred, born from the hope as he approached, a hope that she may respond to his gesture of love but then the hardening calcification of heaviness was all too soon to come back when there was no acknowledgement returned by his dear love.

As he ambled away he tried to make a pact with himself to stop and give Goldbar her space.

This covenant which he would mentally agree with himself then would soon collapse as his heart slid down the slope of a molehill again.

He stared at the grass with a despondency of melancholic sadness. Upon the grass he noticed a train of ants. They pressed forward with military precision. He envied them their purpose and unity seeming devoid of any emotions.

Standing in that field he felt so alone, but the love of his life was just a few meters away under the shade of a yonder mango tree yet she could be on the other side of the world for all the difference it made.

That evening after the sun had retired and the moon was to rise high above by taking its throne amongst the stars, Sileas would sit on her usual spot on the porch beside where Eamon would also once sit on his wicker chair.

Often she would find her hand straying as if to reach out for where his would once have been only then to realise its absence so pulled back her own hand to hold in her lap.

She looked across at the horses. How strange they have been over the past couple of weeks.

Before they both would sleep standing together under that mango tree inseparable, Goldbar resting her head on Dougal's neck, but these recent days and nights they seemed so apart, as if they sensed the grief that had swept across the farm and choose a distance from each other was the requisite.

How can this be? She knew animals were sensitive, but before to prise apart that pair would seem impossible! That curious twinning of a couple of horses who appeared joint at the flanks. Yet now it just did not seem proper in the abstract of her mind that they have ended up so separately apart.

She thought surely they would need each other more if they could sense what happened, the fickle shortness of life and how a true love is all we really can rely upon she thought, but there they appeared, poles apart in affection, a shake of the head to all romantic beliefs when sending up smoke to Eros.

If her Eamon was here he would certainly feel sadly disappointed as he felt a certain pride in their matching since bringing Dougal to the farm.

The thought of her husband threatened to bring more tears to her eyes so she looked around for a distraction.

On the table was the pad of paper which Bell had been drawing upon. The crayons lay close by that she had used to colour the blank pages.

Bell had been quiet these days and Sileas so very wished that she would come out her shell and tell her what she was feeling so as to explore their grief for Eamon together.

Sileas reached across to the table and picked up the paper pad out of idle curiosity.

Squiggles and lines, coloured patches and circles, the typical coloured wax pigmented outpour of any six year old Sileas contemplated to herself but then she turned a page and saw something so very different than the randoms before which preceded it on the white leafs.

There was the yellow sickle of a crescent moon and a sprinkling of crosses signifying stars, nothing exceptional there, but then there was a painstakingly drawn five point star within the crayon constellation which caught her eye.

As an artist herself she knew a child's abilities, especially her own little Bell's and this had exceeded anything her little daughter had drawn before.

At each five corners there was a slight tinted squiggle as if to indicate a curving, the effect was almost three dimensional and the shading added to the result, but what caught Sileas' breath more was the words written underneath which named it as "Papa Star"

Bell never mentioned her papa since his death so to see this drawing meant something beyond mere words alone, it signified a deep unexpressed emotion which was her daughter had released with this art upon the paper.

Sileas felt a tear bead from in her eye and looked up to catch it from running down her cheek then saw the moon was at a waxing crescent as in Bell's drawing.

She looked again from paper to heavens and could see the stars matched up in the night sky as aligned almost perfectly with the page which she then held up for a better comparison.

Just then the tears which he fought so hard to hold in check spilled down her face in wet rivulets when she realised the brightest star in the firmament above mapped perfectly as on the paper was Papa Star!

Bell slept through the call of the rooster that morning so it was almost eight before she climbed out of bed, a long lay in for the youngster but this was getting more common since her father's death as her heart felt heavy and weighted her body so could only find a respite within sleep.

She changed from her pjs into pink shorts and a baggy hoodie before going into the bathroom to brush her teeth.

The upturned green crate with the Antarctica logo which she used for standing on to reach the sink was not there so she spat the paste down the toilet then flushed.

She stepped through to the kitchen and got a glass of milk from the fridge which she drink swiftly without taking time to sit down.

She could not see her mama around, Sileas usually came into the bathroom when she heard Bell was up as to ensure she rinses well after brushing but there was no sign of her this morning.

Bell could see a sadness in her mama since papa had died, it hurt Bell to her core seeing mama so quiet with such heartache, she wished so hard that Mama would brighten, just even a little bit as this would make Bell herself feel much better.

Bell never knew how to approach talking to her mama about her papa so choose to stay silent instead,

Bell stepped outside onto the porch and then saw Mama sitting there on the seat where Papa use to sit.

'Well?' said Sileas to her daughter.

Bell looked at her moma puzzled. 'What is it mama?' she replied a little concerned that she was about to be chastised for something she was not aware yet that she had done.

Sileas stood up from the chair and looked up at the sky shielding her eyes from the already blazing morning sun with her hands.

'Do you know that the stars are still up there is the sky during daytime just as they are at night, but we just don't see them as much because the sun is out too?' Sileas announced.

Bell just looked at her mama with confusion as she was slightly baffled at this statement.

Sileas added whilst turning around to look Bell in the face and clarified 'Just because we no longer see Papa does not mean he is not watching us from up there and down here he would want us to carry a smile on our faces in his memory.'

Bell continued to look at her mama's face and saw there was a big smile developing on it.

Bell's own face then started to tremble at the lips and corrugated around her eyes.

Sileas bent down on her hunkers with arms wide open and tears in her eyes. Bell raced over to be caught in her mother's welcoming grip. They hugged each other tight and the tears flowed in a torrent, not all quite out of sadness but remembrance birthed some of these tears too as did the realisation that neither one was any longer alone on this journey of grieving for the man they both so very much loved and had recently lost.

Once the embrace ended and Sileas dried her own tears and that of Bell's with the corner of her blouse she instructed her daughter, 'You'd better go grab that crate,' pointing to the green upturned Antarctica box at the corner of the porch, 'then go get some braids in our Goldbar's hair, poor Dougal hardly recognises his wife these days.'

Bell broke into the biggest smile which evolved into a grin and then skipped across the porch picking up the crate and the blue ribbons on top with both hands before jumping off the porch towards the field.

'Careful, don't run!' shouted Sileas to Bell's retreating back with a broad smile, but the warning went unheeded as Bell sprinted onwards the open gate of the paddock.

Goldbar raised her head at the sound of Bell approaching.

Here was Bell coming with her crate and trailing the blue ribbons in her hand, this could only mean one thing!

Goldbar's spirits instantly soared. She pawed at the ground with her hoof and her tail swished with excitement at the prospect what was about to happen.

Bell tossed the crate to the ground and lassoed her arms around Goldbar's neck as she bent low as to receive the much needed embrace. Bell delivered a multitude of kisses on her coarse haired cheek. Goldbar was overcome with a feeling of pure elation.

Bell retrieved the crate and placed it upturned at the side of the mare, she climbed aboard then set to work braiding the strands of Goldbar's mane.

'Papa Star is up there watching us so need to make a good job!' she sang out between humming with concentration as we weaved the blue ribbons within the horse's hair, 'and we need to get you pretty again for Mr Dougal!' she added out aloud at which Dougal raised his head hearing his name mentioned across the field.

Goldbar still never looked across at him so Dougal dropped his gaze again back toward the ground with the discouragement that the rejected felt, that renewed glimmer of hope again faded.

Bell was busy humming a tune on her lips whilst knitting the blue ribbons into the braids on Goldbar's mane. The mare was in horse heaven, she was relaxing with the feeling of these small fingers working away at the thatch of her mane, its calmed her to the very soul. She was almost in a trancelike state, such was the relief of the moment.

The all of a sudden Bell let out a scream and tumbled from the crate.

Goldbar's eyes snapped opened with such a fright!

At first she saw Bell lying there, her head had hit the ground so hard from the fall she was stunned motionless and just then Goldbar detected the moment of the rearing viper just a couple of feet away raising itself within it's coil about to aggressively dart another bite at the fallen child, this time it would be aimed at her face which was now within striking distance as the little girl was on the ground.

Goldbar was positioned side on and was desperately attempting to turn as to get between Bell and the viper yet she already knew she would not make the manoeuvre in time nevertheless had to try something but just then a crashing reddish brown bulk railroaded passed her view crashing into the fence post under the mango tree where they were.

It was Dougal, he had propelled himself forward at such a crushing speed that the big horse had no time to break before hitting into the post.

Goldbar's first thought was that the clumsy big oaf could have crushed the little girl but when she looked down there was Bell, still lying on the ground thankfully not trodden on but also was athe mangled remains of the serpent pulverised into the earth by the big Clydesdale's feet.

He had slew the snake under his powerful hooves!

When she looked across at Dougal he was unsteadily lumberingly getting to his feet. He had hit the post which such a force that the wood had broken into two splintered ends which wobbled vigorously still attached to the wire of the fence.

She looked down at Bell again, she was still unmoving on the ground, stunned into unconsciousness from the smack on her head caused by her fall from the crate caused by the viper's attack.

A red welt was developing on her lower leg, the snake must have bite her there causing her to fall.

Goldbar pawed at Bell, Wake up Wake up her actions pleaded. She stuck her nose down to the girls face...Please Wake Up! No movement.

Dougal now tottering on all four hooves crossed over to where Bell lay and clamped the loose material at the top of Bell's hoodie between his teeth then without so much as a pause he started pulling, dragging her out from under the mango tree into the field.

Goldbar ran around neighing as loud as she could trying to get attention from the house but no sign of Sileas.

Dougal continued to haul Bell's unconscious body across the ground with his firm but precision grip on the bundled material of the hoodie pulling her toward to open gate of the field in the direction of the farm house.

As he approached the opening of the paddock he felt that familiar panic arise again, born from his past traumatic experiences with Ludd's punishment, the fear reared like daggers within him threatening with excruciating brutal tortures, but he thought through it, these latent barrier erected up from the depths of his psyche, he crushed them back down just as he had done with the snake. He threw the invisible jockey from his dorsal, this dark cruel rider which was attempting to pull him back, he mentally bucked him like a broken rodeo rider into the air then dragged Bell's little form up towards the farm house through the open gate with Goldbar now racing ahead to get help.

Sileas was at the kitchen sink having just turned off the tap when she heard the commotion from outside. She went out onto the porch to see what the fuss was and there was Goldbar with Dougal behind her dragging something along the ground towards the farm house. It was not something, it was Bell! Dougal had a hold of Bell her mind screamed! The horse has went crazy and had got a hold of Bell!

Sileas grabbed the broom from the porch as ran out barefooted toward the big horse passing a panicking Goldbar on the way.

She screamed in her transit for Dougal to release Bell which he done just as she was closing the gap between them but already she'd swung the broom full pelt in its arch with her own momentum behind it clubbing the big stallion across the head.

Dougal reared away before collapsing on the grass rolling onto his flank heaving deeps breaths with red crimson foam bubbling from his twitching flaring nostrils.

Sileas looks down at her daughter.

Her hoodie was stretched out she could see, luckily the horse had pulled her by only the material. She scanned her little body for any injuries.

Bell started to arouse groggily mumbling sobbingly.

'Mama!' she cried, 'my leg hurts!'

'It's ok baby,' Sileas countered in automatic reply as she triaged her eyes across Bell's slight frame, 'stay still honey!'

Sileas looked down at Bell's legs and saw a red swelling on the meat of her left calf, there were two puncture marks, unmistakably the work of a snake.

She quickly lifted her daughter bundling the little girl in her arms and raced into the house.

Sileas lay her daughter on the couch then scrambled to the fridge getting the anti-venom kit out.

She already knew the exact paediatric dose which would be required silently thanking her stars that she had always took the precaution of reading up before as to be prepared if such an eventuality should it arise.

She slapped a crying Bell's arm pumping the forearm up and down whilst tightly grasping her upper arm to encourage the appearance of a vein before administering the shot via the thin needle intravenously into the thread like blue duct at the crook of her arm.

Bell looked away as the needle entered her arm, continuously cooing in a heartbreaking tone for her mammy.

She'd got the anti-venom in time Sileas thought but still lifted Bell and raced out to the barn to where Eamon's jalopy was kept, she could waste no time harnessing up a buggy, speed of of the essence here so she would use the car to take the girl to get emergency care and get looked over by a doctor, she would leave nothing to chance.

Bell was fully aware now as the fog around her mind from the fall was departing but Sileas commanded her to lay down and try and elevate her lower leg.

Before getting into the car she just remembered they may need to know which type of snake bit her.

It must have been when she was with Goldbar down at the mango tree in the paddock.

Sileas ran down picking up the broom from the grass next to the fallen body of a heavy panting Dougal. She would need the stick to use on the snake to kill it then bring it to the hospital with her for identification.

She was surprised that the big horse was still down, a Clydesdale like that fallen by one blow of a broom across his face, impossible!

When she got under the mango tree she could see immediately this was where the carnage took place.

The ground was scuffed, the post of the fence was broken and leaning at an angle. There on the ground was the mangled remains of a viper amongst large hoof prints. She tossed the broom as no longer requiring a weapon, the snake was well and truly destroyed. She grabbed it's remains to take to the hospital with her to be identified.

She ran back to the car jumping in then soaring out of the barn down the dirt track lane toward the town to take Bell to get her checked over by a doctor.

Already to her relief Bell seemed to be recovering but still better to be safe and get her looked at.

Goldbar stood over Dougal with her head down nuzzling him with desperate caresses.

He was struggling to gain his breath. His chest had took the brunt of the impact with the fence post when he had launched himself like a rocket towards the attacking viper and a concave was unmistakably there upon the breast plate where his sternum was.

His breaths started becoming ever more ragged, his eyes closing as if to fall asleep then opening again with a start.

Please Dougal, don't go, please. You saved Bell you did it Goldbar mewled, my dearest love, stay with me.

Dougal's eyes started to get heavier as he looked up at Goldbar, she saw only love being radiated from his mare and this brought him such peace to his soul. The last sparkle that shone of his closing eyes was a pure love for his soul mare, then they closed for ever as his clunking breathing stopped with a sigh.

Goldbar got down and rested her head across his neck as she use to do before under the mango tree in the evening when they stood together.

Her love was so strong for her stallion then, her heart ached to see him go. Goodbye sweet love she shed out upon the still horse, until me meet again, I love you my Dougal.

By the time Bell was checked out and confirmed to be ok by the doctor, Sileas had pieced together what had actually happened.

She now understood that, to the contrary of what she first believed during the heat of the moment when she had thought that Dougal had actually attacked her daughter. She now came to realise that he was dragging her up to the farm house to get Sileas to assist Bell after he slew the snake by trampling upon it.

She could not bear to think what would have happened if Bell had remained out of her sight for any longer as the venom was taking effect.

Dougal's actions had saved her daughter's life!

Upon returning to the farm Sileas and Bell were received by the saddest of sights.

Poor heroic Dougal lying on the ground had succumbed to his crushed chest and had passed away and there inconsolable Goldbar laying next to the big horse with her head on his neck, her body quivering as if she was sobbing.

She could not be budged away from his side for two days.

The local vet from he village came once they'd got Goldbar back into the paddock and he checked over Dougal's body.

It was certainly the chest injury that was the cause of his death, the horse's sternum had been crushed from the impact with the fence post.

The broom handle smashed across his face would have been a pinprick in comparison to the major trauma of the breast injury but still the guilty of hitting her daughter's saviour stung Sileas deeply.

The vet could not believe the big Clydesdale has been able to move so far with such a devastating injury, especially dragging the weight of a child with him.

Such determination, he had said, heard had he heard of this before in any beast.

When telling this to Sileas she cringed at him calling Dougal a beast, although technically correct, this so called "beast" had saved her daughter whilst sacrificing himself in the process.

One of the neighbouring farmers had a excavator which he kindly drove up to the farm and dug a hole within the paddock just out from under the mango tree and that's was where they buried Dougal, his finally resting place, the same spot where he enjoyed such tender moments with Goldbar when they were together.

There were no markings on the plot but often Bell and Seleas would place a some freshly picked flowers down on the ground and say a few words with shedded tears as Goldbar would stand reverential at their side looking down at the plot of earth.

They often wondered why there would be a small pile of carambola fruit on his grave, they could never understand this but Goldbar knew.

Goldbar was in a deep sadness at the loss of her true love. It lasted a while but eventually with lots of love from both Bell and Sileas she started to improve but the grief left its mark on her and she never seemed the same mare again. In the evenings she still stood alone just by the mango tree beside Dougal's grave.

After some months Seleas noticed Goldbar was putting on some weight around her belly.

She called out the vet who confirmed her suspicions. Goldbar was in foal then seven months later she was to foal a beautiful colt who Bell christened with the name Douglas, a Scottish sounding name in honour of the father Dougal.

Douglas was a health colt albeit a little clumsy but they would see the Clydesdale stock was strong in him and he would grow up to be very strong. Goldbar sadness lifted greatly at this wonderful gift her dear true love had left her.

One evening Sileas saw Bell sitting on her green upturned crate, just out from where the mango tree was. The little girl was staring up at the night sky with her crayons and notepad in her lap. Goldbar with Douglas were standing right next to her, both stretching there heads up to the heavens almost synchronised with Bell.

Sileas, conscious of the evening chill, went out to join her daughter with a blanket to drape across her shoulders then asked her if she was looking for Papa Star up there amongst the vaults of the heavens?

Bell answered in the affirmative then added that Papa was now next to Dougal up there to keep the brave horse company so they both could look down and guard their ladies and the young Douglas.

Bell lifted up the notebook from her lap to show her mammy and right enough, there was a mapped comparison to the constellations of the night sky up above their heads that evening.

Seleas could see that it was actually the Pegasus constellation up there but she never corrected the little girl, just said that yes, she could make out the big Clydesdale's features and true enough, there was Papa star keeping him company too and shining down, guarding, protecting and watching over them all.

Well my little one, stories should always end with a "The End." and this one is no different.

Do you see how from the ashes of grief true love proves itself?

Never underestimate its powers my little one. When Prometheus gave us fire he was already relegated into second place honours after it were Eros, son of Aphrodite who gave us the power to love and its that love which continues to warm the heart once the flames of a fire die.

I know you don't understand little one but one day you will, one day you will cry and feel the beating of your heart so strong it will threaten to burst forth out of your chest. You will neigh up to the heavens for just one more chance.

You may give freshly pulled roses and receive kissing nuzzles in return or you may lay carambolas in the hope that she may respond, but you will, I promise, one day surely experience love, the joys and the pains and the memories.

But let's not discuss that just now, that's a discussion for another day.

Now what you may ask became of Goldbar, well memories have a tendency to heal even the most broken of hearts and with the knowledge of the old farmer Eamon and Dougal looking down upon her she she found her happiness again with the memories left and the legacy of her true love Dougal then presented to her with their son Douglas.

One day you will tell this tale to your little one wither he'd be a colt or a filly. What is that you say? The floating bark will maybe a splinter by then and be swallowed whole by a big fish? Ha, perhaps this story is not as old as I would pretend my dear one, maybe the talk of tractors, excavators, jalopies and anti-venoms gives that game away that it happened during my own lifetime, perhaps it was not passed down to me by my momsicle and popsicle, perhaps it was earlier that I pretend!...then does that mean I am the author of this tale?

Some tales don't need authors my dear, some tales can just be recounted like a memory, a sweet dear precious memory.

Now that's enough for for tonight my dear boy, your auld grandnannie here is feeling tired and does not have that spring in her hooves as she once did when she was younger when she had a golden mane not this silver you now see in her twilight years.

I feel like an evening snack so perhaps I will take a wander out to yonder tree and pick some starfruit off its branches.

What is starfruit you may ask, well we once knew them as carambolas when we were younger.

Maybe I will tell you more in the morning, perhaps about your grandbubbie who passed before you were born, just as your own father's father died before he was foaled.

Did I ever tell you that you that your father was named in honour of him? Yes, that same name your own father passed down to you!

But off to bed with you now young Douglas, this auld palomino needs her beauty sleep.

FROM THE HORSE'S MOUTH

Nowadays I am but a constellation upon the tapestry which you observe in your night sky.

A beacon to navigators, a muse of dreamers or a candle for lovers.

A grouping of stars on a celestial sphere as was the homage the great Zeus rewarded me upon my accent after my service to him and others.

It's from here, from this constellations in which my consciousness is stabled, I look down upon you all from 34,000 light-years away.

Mine is the seventh largest constellation to be seen as you view your night sky, so easy enough to spot if you have the inclination and patience.

When I was to be transformed into my constellation a single feather from my wings drifted gently down to earth then landed next to a town called Parthenia which then was to be called the city of Tarsus.

The biblical name Tarsus means "Winged Feather."

It were to be the birth place of the saint that Christianity calls Paul the apostle who was also known as Saul of Tarsus.

Do you see how religions and what your historians called myths are all linked? It were Dionysus who first turned water into wine.

Was it not your own modern day Homer, the one named William that had once wrote that there are more things in Heaven and Earth than are dreamt of in your philosophy?

I can tell you that this is true, and that the renderings of certain more modern scriptures have a lot to thank the tales of my own time for.

I constantly hear my story told and retold over many a hearth to Hestia's delight, but much has since changed through the years in its retellings.

Such as my relation to Perseus, which has been much misrepresented by thespians and scribes down the aeons in order to deliver dramatics for your stage then later to your flicker shows on cinematic screens.

Some errors of truth have been less pretentious than others and there has been sincere mistakes snowballing over time like a game of Chinese Whispers, but here I am now to tell you the facts, my own accounts, straight from the horse's mouth so to speak.

Firstly let me clear up the most irritating of all the contrivances which cause my ears to prick back with annoyance.

That vexation is the tales about a certainly Perseus and what many people consider his relationship to me.

Let me be clear about this, my only connection to Perseus during these times of past was that he killed my mother, an event which was instrumental in my birth, so as such he is as much an accessory to my own tale as an obstetrician is to a grown man.

But perhaps I should mention about my mother first and within the telling also divulge my father's role of his immoral encounter with her.

My mother was another person of much legendary account but not deemed the most gallant variety of such, although I daresay you do not know her true story and so you will surely judge her unfairly.

Her name was Medusa, ahhh, I almost see that you recognise the name and I suspect the connection you are making is that of the Gorgon with a crown of hissing serpents, being green of hide with a slithering rattling snake's tail and a gaze which turned many a man into a pillar of stone. Yes, that is true, that is what she became, but listen and allow me to divulge to you more.

She was not always that way as once she was a stunning young woman with beautiful ringlets of hair and an alluring beauty which frustrated many a suitor as she'd dedicated herself as a priestess to the house of the goddess Athena and as such took a vow of chastity.

Such was her then exquisite beauty that the Roman writer Ovid was to praised her once ravishing hair as "the most wonderful of all her charms."

He hair was as red as the tresses that crowned upon the great Athena and even a greater compliment could be had with a comparison to that of the perfect Aphrodite herself, as Botticelli would depict as her image standing upon the shell.

"But they were blonde" I hear you declare! Ha, how easily influenced you are by these modern days my friends.

During the great epoch when I flew the sky blonde hair was associated with prostitutes, those loose woman who coloured their hair the hint of straw with saffron dyes to attract customers. Would you dare class my mother as such?

In your modern days red hair has its distractors but in my day it was the symbol of sensuality and had a sexual promiscuity, just look at the Pre-Raphaelites and Titans who knew of its allure.

Nowadays red hair is still a bestowed gift upon people, it acts like a filter attracting the more interesting towards the owner.

I'm sure Hepburn and Hayworth would agree yet the modern child gets teased so much whilst in his youth whilst sporting red locks! By Zeus, how times change, but not for the better I may add, but I digress, back to the tale.

As I already said, she was an avowed priestess of Athena but then her beauty was to catch the eye of my father-to-be who was Poseidon and he was to desired her greatly but could not have her due to her solemn vows which she'd taken to preserve her maidenhood in her service to Athena.

Poseidon, the God of the seas would not allow this to desist him so he went on to ravage her against her will when he was to find her attending Athena's shrine.

Like many women of ancient times, she was a victim of a patriarchal society, perhaps not all that different from these days do I hear you say?

Well, once the foul deed had been done Poseidon took his leave after which the virgin Goddess Athena was to find out.

She was so enraged at the defilement which happened inside her own temple and that one of her own priestesses had defied her chastity vows the goddess wanted redress.

As Athena could not very well seek revenge on a fellow god, such as Poseidon was, so her wrath had to be served upon Medusa the innocent victim.

The vengeful goddess was to transform Medusa's enchanting red hair into a coil of snakes, then twisted her features into that of a monster giving her tusks and a brass claw upon the end of each finger.

Her skin was turned a greenish hue and she was given the serpent's forked tongue. Her eyes were to remain beautiful but the curse would be that anyone who were to gaze upon them would be turned to instantly to stone.

Medusa was then, as the great poet Virgil's unkind written words would describe of her "an enormous monster about whom snaky locks twist their hissing mouths"

Despite the undeserved punishment which the classic case of unfair victim blaming dished upon her by Athena, my mother's heart remained untouched such was its purity and kindness.

As she did not wish to harm a human soul with the curse of her gaze, she ran away to a cave as to seek a life of solitude away from others, but others would never allow her to live such a quiet life as they would seek her out in the attempt to prove themselves heroes by their endeavours to slay "the monster!"

Perseus was one such "hero" as he were to cut off my mother's head whilst she were asleep.

He done his hacking with an adamantine sword gifted to him from the gods. A sickle like weapon which was a perfect replica of the one which Cronos used on his father, a dark murderous tool for a dark murderous task.

Another factcheck I wish to raise at this juncture is that, unlike some stories will have it, I was not born from when the blood dripped from my mother's snake haired decapitated head as it touched water during Perseus' fleeing with his gruesome prize in a sack, although it was not unusual that from such horrors delivering the most beautiful, as the birthing of the great Aphrodite will testify as her fully grow form materialised within a great foaming when Ourano's castrated genitals hit the ocean just after Cronos gilded him and threw the departed organs into the brine.

But no, although my foaling could be still deemed as almost just as horrific as I was to spring from the spurting neck-stump of my mother's decapitation whilst the "hero" Perseus winging away on the flying sandals lent to him from the god Hermes, images of which artisans from the Archaic period would go on to depict upon their amphora vases.

* * *

Upon my birthing I was to ascend bolting up into the sky threshing my wings and there I did fly and not to stop until I reached the top of the heights of Mount Helicon where as my hoofs stuck the earth upon my landing water was to burst forth which was then to become what was known as The Hippocrene Spring, translated as horse spring.

This would then become the waterhole that would be favoured by the Muses, these divinities who presided over songs, stories, poetry, and the arts.

It was said that anyone drinking from these waters would feel a wave of poetic inspiration flood across them.

Your poet John Keats would write of such within his Ode To a Nightingale.

Perseus would then go on to defeat a Cetus whilst wearing these winged sandals using my mother Medusa's head as a weapon holding it forth turning the gigantic beast into a pillar of stone this saving his bride-to-be, the beautiful Princess Andromeda.

You will observed that the creature as I have just mentioned as "a Cetus" and not the Kraken as certain movies would wrongly claim. "Release the Kraken" is a particular soundbite you surely will have heard I would wager? The scribes who wrote such on the scripts were wrong in both geography and era.

The Kraken is a Norse myth of a later time, a sea beast which attacked ships off the Norwegian coast.

Yet perhaps the Norwegian Kraken could be classed as a Cetus as this is a description of a multitude of sea beasts but under no stretch could this particular Cetus which Perseus was to slay be called a Kraken. If they do so then it's certainly not the Hippocrene fountain they have drunk from, more likely to have been in their cups with Dionysus!

The only other tie I have with Perseus is that I am up here in his family of constellations.

Up on this ceiling Perseus still holds my mother's severed head forever as an eternal capture of his murderous act, but I hold no lasting grudge against him truth be told.

Let us not judge too harshly on this slayer of the sea beast and hero of Aethiopia, as in his heart did beat a great love for young Andromeda which drove him to the act out of necessity to obtain a weapon to deal with such a sea beast.

The truth of a love must mark a man and top his legacy over all other things he has done.

Nae I hold no grudge agains Perseus, his mission was to save his loved one and by then my mother Medusa was already so cursed that death came as a blessed relief for her.

As with myself, the particular Cetus of that tale is also up here belonging to the Perseus family of constellations.

We also share it with Andromeda, Cassiopeia who was Andromeda's mother, Cepheus the father of Andromeda and of course young Perseus himself.

Then there is also within this same array of stars is Auriga who was a famous horse trainer.

Auriga was also known as Erichthonius of Athens.

As with my own birthing, Erichthonius' etching into existence was not a glamorous event either.

He came into being when the goddess Athena visited the blacksmith god Hephaestus to request him to forge some weapons for her, but Hephaestus was so overcome by lusty desire that he tried to seduce the great Athena right there in his workshop.

Athena, determined to maintain her virginity fought him off but during their struggle Hephaestus' ejaculated seed fell upon her thigh. In her disgust she wiped it off with a scrap of sheep's wool then tossed it to the earth.

Erichthonius was born from that seed which hit the earth.

The name Erichthonius in Greek means "troubles born from the earth."

Athena did not want anyone to find out about this secret child so she placed him in a small box and then gave him away to the three daughters of the then King of Athens instructing them never to look into the box.

The sisters eventually defied the goddess' command so would open the box and there they discovered the tiny baby, the sight of which drove two of them so insane that they flung themselves to their death from the top of the Acropolis!

Erichthonius would eventually grow out of the small box then into a man raised by the third sister.

He would go on to become the King of Athens and was much loved by his people. He would teach them how to yoke horses and use them to pull chariots, a skilled I suspect he inherited from Athena.

Then he went on the teach them how to smelt silver and to till the earth with a plough, knowledge surely within his DNA from his father's side.

He was also lame of his foot just as Hephaestus was so this handicap motivated him to invented the four-horse chariot to aid him getting around more easily.

It is said he went on to compete as a chariot driver in games and Zeus so impressed with his skills that he raised him to the heavens to become the constellation of Auriga, also to be known as the Charioteer after his death.

Now as I mentioned before, it were not Perseus who would mount upon on my back and with who I would ride into adventures. No, it was to be a young Prince from Corinth by the name of Bellerophon who would have that great honour.

Bellerophon's mother was Eurynome and she seemed always to be in the favour of the gods, particularly Athena who taught Eurynome much wisdom, but not enough it seems, to avoid a dalliance with my father Poseidon.

Some rumours even have it that Poseidon, not King Glaucus was Bellerophon's true father which later events would prove most likely the case, at least in Poseidon's mind, and if this is true then it would make us half-brothers which certainly would go a long way to explain my bond with him.

Bellerophon, grandson of the boulder rolling Sisyphus, did indeed capture me as I drank from my favoured watering hole but he needed help from the gods to do so.

Bellerophon, although he was a great equestrian still needed some magic to ensnare and tame me during these days of my wild youth.

That magic was to come to him in the form of the gift of a charmed golden bejewelled bridle gifted by the goddess Athena for that very purpose to be used upon I.

His possession of such a present from the gods came about after he first consulted with a wise man called Polyidus who told him to sleep in the temple of Athena, that very same temple I had been conceived in when Poseidon raped my mother.

Once asleep in the temple, after evening prayers to Athena,

Bellerophon dreamt of me, this great white winged horse. Then upon wakening he was to find in his hands the enchanted bridle he was to use upon me.

Wild and free-roaming I was when I bent to drink water from my favoured Peirene spring on the top of the Acrocotinth.

Bellerophon stealthy crept up behind me then slipped the magic bridle over my head before climbing up onto my back.

Then with a great panic I spread my wings and flew up into the sky trying to shake this impertinent intruder off from my back.

He held on as tight as grim death and soon I was brought under control by him. I say him, but in truth it was more due to the seduction of the magic bridle than the horsemanship of Bellerophon himself such was its power, but we did bond and I was to became his faithful stallion.

You can certainly read Bellerophon's tale yourself in the Iliad but I will tell you about it from my own mouth here and how our adventures together came about.

Let it never be said that my friend Bellerophon was not an honourable man for that he was and when the wife of King Proetus, Queen Stheneboea (Homer was to call her Queen Anteia in his writings within the Iliad), tried to seduce him he rejected her advances.

It is often said that Hell hath no fury like a woman scorned and I know this a true one as the Queen then started to make up prevarications about him telling her husband the King that Bellerophon had tried to seduce her.

In actual fact she was falsifying the seduction in the opposite direction.

King Proteus believing his Queen sent Bellerophon away to Lycia to met the Proteus' father-in-law, King Iobates.

Bellerophon with the innocence of youth was not aware of the lies Stheneboea had spoke into the King's ears so he happily went as instructed to visit King Iobates bearing a sealed message for the King to be delivered on the request of Proteus.

The message from Proteus to Iobates, the contents which Bellerophon was unaware, told King Iobates to kill his young visiting guest due to his attempted ravishment of Stheneboea (this was also the origin of the expression a "Bellerophonic letter")

Before reading the message King Iobates warmly received his guest then eagerly opened the received letter to read the latest news from his son-in-law King Proetus.

Upon reading it he understood what had been asked of him, he was to dispatch of the young Bellerophon.

Iobates was worried, to kill this young man would be violating a rule in Greek culture which was not to treat guests badly, this would surely make the god's angry with him.

Guest-host relationships were much valued amongst the gods, especially Zeus.

Iobates remembered all too well as to what befell Troy when Paris abducted the wife of King Menelaos of Sparta.

What was Iobates to do?

A conundrum indeed. Risk the wrath of the gods or lose the respect of his son-in-law King Proetus.

Iobates's answer was to let fate decide so he sent Bellerophon on a mission with tremendous danger.

He asked the young man to kill the beast which was known as the Chimera which has causing havoc by burning down local villages and slaughtering the inhabitants.

Vanity and pride were two things Bellerophon had in abundance so he eagerly accepted the request to banish the beast.

In the Iliad Homer described the Chimera as…"in the fore part a lion, in the hinder a serpent, and in the midst a goat, breathing forth in terrible wise the might of blazing fire" and from my memory I would say he was not far off the mark with such a description.

The Chimera was a hybrid monster, she was made up of the body parts of a lion, a goat, and a snake. She, yes as the Chimera was indeed female.

The name Chimera comes from the Greek word chimaira, meaning "she-goat."

She had three heads, luckily only the goat's head was the one which breathed fire, if all three heads did then I think our adventures would not have progressed past that point, small mercies such as they were.

At the front she had the head of a lion then spouting from the middle of her back was that fire breathing head of a goat then the tail ended in the venomous head of a snake, a terrible sight to behold!

Her devilish looks were not surprising as she was the offspring of the equally monstrous Typhon and Echidna, and as such a predictable result of such a hideous pairing.

To defeat the Chimera Bellerophon needed to hatch a plan so he met with Polyidus again to discuss a strategy.

Athena also came to him in a dream warning him that the Chimera could only be defeated from above, a task which could be easier contemplated when you had a flying horse in your corner I would have thought.

The day came when we set off with Bellerophon riding high on my back with a clutch of spears at his side.

Up and on we did soar, searching from a high over the lands of Lycia until we found the dreaded Chimera.

I circled the beast from above dipping low so Bellerophon could gouge it with the tip of his spear.

Due to the density of its armoured hide the spear did little damage but the creature's blood did run and as green as the grass it did appear.

Eventually we flew up high again to prepare for another diving attack upon the monster during which time, in preparation Bellerophon attached a ball of lead to the tip of his spear.

We swooped downward for the attack.

The Chimera saw our approach then opened the cavernous well of one of its gigantic mouths, the goat's head as to breath out fire and at that moment Bellerophon took his cue.

He launched his lead tipped spear into the great orifice of the creatures mouth where it sank in deep and true whereas the lead turned molten from the colossal heat and ran down its throat, sliding deep down before then solidifying again within the monstrous neck. The inner vital organs stiffened as the lead congealed into hardness strangulating the creature from within and putting an end to its days of terrifying rein.

We flew back to the city returning victorious to a welcoming reception as the conquering heroes.

Garlands of flowers were placed around my neck and flasks of wine were handed to Bellerophon who was then named as the slayer of beasts.

Oh how he celebrated that joyful evening whereas, forever the cautious one, I were to look past his boasts to where I could see King Iobates contemplating the situation and then hatching other plans to put to young Bellerophon, such was the churning thoughts I believe were taking form in his head.

Indeed my suspicions were soon to be proven true and the party was short lived as the King elicited Bellerophon aid again the very next morning as he asked him to defeat another of his enemies.

This new challenge was to be the Amazons who lived near the city of Themiskyra by the banks of the Thermodon River, in a country I believe you now call Turkey.

They were a tribe of warrior woman who fought more fearsomely than men.

It's my understanding that your modern culture sees a romantic notion with these battling woman, a femme fatale of the Hollywood era with such as the Wonder Woman superhero but let me clear this other fallacy of your modern age before we proceed.

The first Amazonian woman, Otrera as was her name, she was born the offspring of a coupling between Ares the god of war and an Akmonian wood nymph called Harmonia.

Ares blood ran strong and fierce within her veins and continued such a course with her decedents which was to be many.

The tribe she raised grew and multiplied into an army of warrior women who only raised daughters after using the male slaves for their seed.

Any newborn male babies were either executed on the spot or if appeared to be sturdy enough they were placed into slavery.

Ha…the ultimate extreme feminist I hear you say and perhaps spoken truly.

The name Amazon makes most contemporary minds think of that winding river in South America, but the term was from an old script, the classical Greek word "Amazoi" which means breast-less as whilst a girl in the tribe was still a child and yet to reach maturity, her right breast would be removed using a red hot sizzling bronze blade which would then also cauterise the wound with its searing heat.

This was thought to be a necessary mutation as to remove any possible hinderances for her using a spear or drawing an arrow during battle such was their commitment to being the ultimate warriors.

Quoting Homer, again in his Iliad described them as "woman who go to war like men" and he was once again on the mark as he was with his description of the Chimera.

As was the historian Heredotus when he called them "Androktones" which means "killers of men", perhaps a killer of winged horses too I would consider at the time so was very wary about facing such a foe.

It was said that during the battle of Troy the Amazons sided with the Trojans lead by the Amazon Queen Penthesilea who was slain by Achilles.

Only when he removed her helmet did he realised she was a woman. Such was his disgust that a woman should have put up such a challenge in battle that he then desecrated her still warm corpse in a much worse way to what he was later to do to a dead Hector.

You can perhaps use your imagination here, then you will certainly understand why this scene never made it into the Hollywood movie!

I always carried great respect for these warrior woman, a factor was their agility on horseback which was as legendary as were their skills in combat so it was with some reluctance I took Bellerophon high to the skies on my back that day to deliver their demise.

The strategy was to drop the largest rocks we could gather by hoisting them up upon my flanks with vine ropes, then to drop them from up high upon their tribal settlement before collecting more.

This proved to be a deadly bombardment.

It was a misty morning when we started the bombing, up high enough not to be hit by any arrows which they blindly released skyward into the gloom, and that mist lasted until late afternoon on the day of the battle which would lead me to believe the gods were on our side.

The stragglers from the tribe who did not get mash from the plummeting rocks above attempted to flee into the surrounding forests only to be taken out by Iobate's men who lay in wait for such their opportunity.

Unknown to us at the time some Amazons did escape by swimming down the river. This I am thankful for as I hate the idea of a genocide.

I much later learnt that the Amazons, although much depleted, carried their race for many generations to come.

An Amazon Queen called Thalestris was later to attempt a union with Alexander the Great. They spent thirteen nights together making love but no seed did take and Thalestris eventually died without an heiress.

There are still some descendants from the great Amazon clan, I observe them from above these days with respect instead of raining down rocks upon their heads.

They still have a passion for horses and show bravery. A man can easily loss his heart to such a woman, I have seen it many a time, but once again I transgress…back to this tale of Bellerophon.

It was a cowardly victory in my thoughts, attacking from a distance in height and not seeing the whites of our foe's eyes but as they were prone to defend from the ground, an attack from above had been an unexpected tactic delivering a victory nevertheless and Bellerophon celebrated it with great gusto as usual.

Settle I would tell him, this is not a deed to rejoice but a celebrating youth makes no distinction in a win so party that evening he did whilst King Iobate sat thoughtfully on his throne again.

King Iobate was in an other conundrum then.

He had started to like the young man yet had promised King Proteus that he would seal Bellerophon's fate which he had indeed attempted by sending him on increasingly dangerous missions but every time Bellerophon would return victorious, surely the gods must look upon this young man with favour, but the King noticed that he boasted drunkenly after his victories as if he were one of the gods himself, never a good idea as can invoke the anger of the true deities high up on Mount Olympus.

Iobate then decided to follow through on his promise to Proteus and send Bellerophon on another mission but this time he would stack the odds even more against the young man by arranging his own personal highly trained guards to ambush him on route.

The next morning Bellerophon set off at a gallop on my back over the land. We had decided to give my wings a rest such was the intensity of the flying with such heavy loads the day before.

The mission requested by King Iobate was to rid his kingdom of the plague which was the Carian pirates who were led by a warrior of no great talent called Cheirmarrhus.

A seeming simpler task than that the previous feats but on-route in a between two high dunes near the sea Iobate's guards set an ambush and were to take us by surprise.

Then instantly, as they sounded their attack, a massive tsunami of water breached out from the ocean and swept between the dunes washing the soldiers out to sea but sparing Bellerophon and myself.

This was a grace that only the great god of the ocean Poseidon himself could conjure!

Remember as I mentioned before, Bellerophon and I may have shared the same father so this was seemingly a blessing which he bestow on both his sons that very moment of our need.

Bellerophon on my back returned to Lycia to confront King Iobate who upon learning what had happened was then to believed beyond any doubts that Bellerophon had the favour of the gods and also realised from this that King Proteus must have been wrong to believe such an honourable young man in the eye of the gods would seduce his Queen.

The King immediately made good the wrongs he done against Bellerophon by giving him the most fertile lands in his kingdom and then making him his heir by offering the hand of his beautiful daughter Princess Philonoe.

Bellerophon's marriage to Philonoe was a fruitful one, she bore him four children. Two boys, Laodameia and Deidameia, and two girls, Hippololochus and Isander.

Despite this richness, land and family Bellerophon still could never console himself to the quiet life, he wanted more.

With his great victories in battle he thought with reflection, he surely himself must be the equal to that of a god and this led to his downfall, literally and figuratively as you will hear.

One fine day and with the courage of too much good wine and the prompting of bad friends, he decided the time had came for him to ascend upwards on my back to Mount Olympus where he thought he'd be welcomed with open arms, then to take his rightful place at the table of equals with the god, a terrible idea to think above your station thus goading the gods.

Up he flew on my back, higher and high ignoring my plights and would not listen to my horse sense of advice that he was committing a terrible mistake.

The great Zeus observed Bellerophon actions with anger that a mortal could consider himself such an equal to the mighty gods of

Mount Olympus so he sent forth a gadfly which stung my rear quarters causing me to buck off Bellerophon from my back in an uncontrollable reaction then send him tumbling to the ground where he was to meet his death hitting the earth.

The all knowing Zeus reined me in and allowed me to serve him by carrying his thunderbolts, a service I did proudly and commendably so as an eternal reward he gave he immortality making me into a constellation as you see in the northern night sky, up there in the hemisphere boreal or what the Chinese call in the Black Tortoise of the North.

There is some telling of the tale that Bellerophon survived his fall back down to earth by landing in a thorny bush of brambles.

That then he was blinded and injured upon landing so that day forth he wandered the lands looking for his family who he never found.

A punishment for trying to claim the powers of the gods.

To this day the fruit of the thorny bramble bush represents arrogance. You may remember this from the thorny crown placed upon Christ's head when the Roman's were to deal with what they'd thought to be his pretensions at being a king.

Later in life during my service to Zeus I was to find love myself. Her name was Ocyrrhoe but I use to call her Euippe which from Ancient Greek means "good mare" and that she was.

She bore me two children, Malanippe and Celeris.

Ocyrrhoe was named after the river where she was born.

Her mother's name was Charicola and was one of the daughters of Apollo. Her father was Chiron who was the king of the centaurs , he is also a constellation up here in the night sky too named as the constellation of Centaurus.

Ocyrrhoe was in human shape during her youth, a nymph as the centaurian blood of her father never took mastery but she did have the gift of prophecy and foretold the fate of her father to him.

The anger of her father upon hearing this was great and he was driven with a vengeance towards his daughter.

She then hide and prayed to Artemis asking her to metamorphose her into a horse so her father could not find her.

Artemis delivered her wish and turned her into a horse, a mare and that was the shape she was when we met and fell in love.

We are still together up here in my constellation, you can see the mare's head behind mine as she still hides at my rear from her father, concealing herself from his Centaurus constellation.

My love Ocyrrhoe's father Chiron was actually quite peaceful for a centaur if you were to overlook him trying to kill his own daughter of course.

That race of creatures who were part horse and part man were known for their violence, lust and savage tendencies but Chiron did not follow this norm, a distinction which ancient artisans would make when depicting him on vases as they would paint him often as having a full human body with just own two horse feet behind as to contrast him from his more barbarous cousins.

Chiron was known for his wisdom too, his enlightened intellect.

He was skilled in many arts, including medicine, gymnastics, prophecy, hunting and music. As such he was later to become a tutor for the mighty Achilles.

He was to teach Achilles how to hunt, heal and which herbs to give as to fight against infection.

The Greek origin of Chiron's name means "skilled with hands", the english word "surgeon" comes from this too, "Cheir" meaning hand and "Ergon" which means work. The word chirurgeon morphed onto surgeon after a few centuries of misspelling.

The much quoted chronicler Homer wrote that Chiron was the "wisest and most just of all Centaurs" and from what I knew of my father-in-law I would agree, well perhaps not so much with the just part, it does not exactly signal of integrity when someone searches for their own daughter with murderous intent even with the reason being that she told her father her prophecy that his death would come about after he would forsake his own immortality to be spared the eternal agonising pain of a serpent's poison. Some people really do struggle with bad news.

Chiron's death was to eventually come about when his skin was accidentally pricked by one of Heracles' poisoned arrows during a visit one day.

The arrow had the poison of the blood of the Hydra on its tip, the nastiest of all venoms. The poison's virulence would make the wound incurable.

Despite Chiron's skill in healing, my father-in-law was fated to an eternity of agony due to the perpetuity of this immortality.

Chiron went to the great Zeus on Mount Olympus were he then offered to give up his immortality in exchange for the freedom of Prometheus who Zeus had chained to the cliff face of the Caucasus Mountains as punishment going against the god's wishes when he gave the gift of fire to mankind.

Chiron had an empathy with Prometheus as this rebellious titan was to suffer also due to his own immortality.

Being chained to that high cliff wall, a vulture would appear at dawn every morning to rip out his liver then devour the organ. His liver would then be regenerated by the next morning for the cycle to be repeated forever more, such was the punishment set for defying the mighty Zeus.

The king of the gods agreed with Chiron's request. He freed Prometheus and made Chiron mortal as to die and end the suffering brought on by the Hydra toxin.

Upon Chiron's death Zeus was to immortalise him once again as he'd done with myself when he placed the centaur's soul among the stars, where he then became the constellation I mentioned before, that which is called Centaurus.

But don't confuse Chiron's Centaurus with the more warlike centaur up there also in the heavens represented by the zodiacal constellation called Sagittarius, they are very different.

Sagittarius up there amongst the stars is demonstrating well the warlike nature of the centaurs as he has his taunt bow drawn with arrow aimed right at the heart of Antares (Anti-Ares) who was a rival of Ares.

Antares is now the bright red heart of Scorpius, the scorpion which Sagittarius takes aim at.

It is said that the centaur archer is avenging Orion, who was slain by the scorpion's sting.

Orion was my half-brother as we shared the same father Poseidon so you can see that it's quite a family we have up here in the stars.

Orion's two faithful dogs are up here too, both Canis Major and Canis Minor.

The Horsehead Nebula is also up here within the constellation of

Orion.

It was my father Poseidon who created the very first horse, yet at that time he had not made what was be come the greatest assistant to mankind for the most honourable of motives.

He created the first horse as a gift for the goddess of agriculture who went by the name Demeter and who he wanted to court behind his wife Amphitrite's back, so the first horse to be brought into being as begot to aid an adulterous god to pursue an unwilling recipient of his lecherous intents. You see? The horse of Troy was not the first equine offering with unscrupulous intentions!

Demeter was also Poseidon's sister, but incest among gods was never unusual, even the great Zeus was wed to his own sister Hera.

As such Demeter would attempt to ward off her brother's advances yet still did not want to incur his wrath.

She came up with a plan.

In an attempt to distract him from his amorous obsession over her she would ask of him too create the most beautiful living creature knowing that the sea god did enjoy a challenge.

Poseidon accepted this gauntlet which Demeter threw down thinking to himself how would she possibly be able to spur his advances if he were to succeed.

He had experienced such success before by creating new creatures into existence to woo woman, one such time was when he created the first dolphin which he then successful used to gain Amphitrite when she had refused his offer of marriage.

As a reward for the dolphin he made it into a constellation which he could do just as well as his brother Zeus.

Delphinus is the name of this small constellation of stars in the northern celestial hemisphere.

He would use the foam from the ocean as his modelling clay.

But this task was proving more difficult than he'd first anticipated.

During his crafting he was to forge more creatures than he had intended but none turned out to be what the perfectionist within him would ever consider the most beautiful creature ever.

He did feel that he was getting close upon his creation of the zebra yet next came the donkey which looked far off the mark.

Eventually his eureka moment had arrived and he was satisfied with his creation...the horse!

He then with great haste went on to create multitude to populate the earth as to show off his greatness to Demeter such was his excitement driven by his unquenchable lust for her.

Upon realising her brother Poseidon achieved the results in a much expedited timescale than what she'd hoped it would take him as she had wishfully though that during his endeavours that itch of desire may have found another victim, preferably a willing one but now she knew that this was not to be.

She knew the only option left was to run away quickly and hide so he would not be able to find her.

She transformed herself into one of the new animals which her brother had created thinking this would be his last guess to what she would do.

She altered her physical form into that of a mare then joined a herd of horses to help aid her disguise, but the all knowing Poseidon saw through his sister's deception so became a stallion himself, then he was to captured and take her by force just as he was later to do with my mother Medusa.

With that encounter, he fathered two of Demeter's children, namely Despoina and Arion.

Despoina was the goddess of mysteries and as such Despoina was not the goddess' real name, that would only be revealed to her true worshipers who were initiated within the Eleusinian mysteries, one of which would be the Despoina cult.

Her brother Arion was born as a horse.

As you can surely imagine from his pedigree my half-brother was to be no ordinary black stallion. He was endowed with a miraculous swiftness of speed and he could also talk.

A talking horse you may say with mocking tone, yet is that not what I am? I also had wings too which Arion did not, I could soar around the skies before I was to take my place in the heavens. You must remember these times of antiquity were also times of enchantment so don't measure them by contemporary rationality.

Earlier we spoke of a Chimera with three head so a horse that can speak surely is much more plausible I would think!

* * *

Homer, that scrivener I quote so often from, he was to describe Arion as a "swift horse…of heavenly stock."

Arion was best known as the horse who saved the life of Adrastus the King of Argos during the war of the Seven against Thebes.

King Adrastus took up the cause of Polynices who was the son of the mother marrying Oedipus, so as such Polynices was supposedly to be the next in line to the throne after the exile of his father but his twin Eteocles took over then banishes his brother Polyneices from Thebes (which is now an area within Luxor and Karnak in Egypt.)

Polyneices would then go off to Argos and raise an army which was to be commanded by seven champions, hence the name, The Seven against Thebes, the original Magnificent Seven story.

The battle was to be a disaster for Polynices' men and only Adrastus was to survive thanks to Arion's lightening speed getting the king to safe ground as the other six champions, including Polynices met with their fates.

I have much to recall about the stories of the past and how they influence the times of the present.

As you can see from these tales my equine cousins feature heavily in the histories of an ancient Greece yet still I only skim the surface.

I have not touched upon one of the most famous and that is the Trojan horse.

Never have I mentioned the famous horses of Achilles, Balius and Xanthos, offspring of the harpy, Podarge and the West wind, Zephyrus.

Missed in my tellings were the nightmarish tales of the mares of Diomedes, which were fed on human flesh and had a prominent role within the labours of Hercules.

Neither did I touch on the Hippocampi who had the upper body of a horse with the lower body of a fish and were used by my father Poseidon to draw his sea-chariot across the ocean.

If I were to tell you about these beasts then I could go on the mention about the small marine fish which are called seahorse that were also sacred to Poseidon.

Their scientific name is Hippocampus, from the ancient greek "Hippos" meaning horse and "Kámpos" meaning monster.

Legend has it that seahorses protect sailors while in the sea.

Greeks believed that when sailors drowned, seahorses escorted them between the physical and spiritual world, this was to ensure no further suffering was to be had during the transition.

In neuroscience the hippocampus is a structure hidden within the temporal lobe of the brain, it's the part which consolidates new memories and weighs out possible outcomes.

It were in the 1500's that the anatomist Giulio Cesare Aranzio observed these horns located alongside the ventricles of the brain and then decided to call them "hippocampi' conceding their resemblance to the seahorse.

As I said, there are many stories in Greek fable with horses but equines also play important roles in the tales from other lands and times too.

Kelpies which were Celtic water horses, King Arthur's mare Llamrei, Nótt's horses Skinfaxi and Hrímfaxi from Norse times not to forget Odin's eight legged horse Sleipnir!

There are more tales of horses and how they helps shape legends and make heroes, more than there are constellations up here in the vaults of heavens and each and every tale is one worth listening to and marvel at.

OLD MAN AND ROSE

The old man did not wanted to leave his wife but it was getting late and the graveyard gates were soon to be closed.

He still had a walk ahead to get himself home back to the empty cottage which awaited him and his aged legs were not the steadiest these days.

'Well my old Maude,' he addressed his wife's headstone out loud as was his tendency during these visits, 'I'd best get myself up that road. I've got a pot of soup to heat on the hob tonight before I get tucked up into bed.'

There was a patch of soil at the front of the grave stone. The old man planted sunflower seeds there every year but they never took, nothing seemed to want to grow in that earth.

Sunflowers were Maude's favourite so it would be so nice to have some around her grave he'd always thought.

The spot was in direct sunlight most of the day and surface of the soil appeared loose enough for any tap roots to take ahold yet still nothing appeared, the seeds did not sprout.

He was disappointed with that.

Perhaps the soil was not alkaline enough he would consider.

Ah well, not to worry, I will be planted here myself one day soon with any luck he commiserated with acceptance.

Such a thought would be macabre to most but to the old man it was almost a comfort, a solemn contemplation of that one day coming when he would be reunited with his dear wife even although only in death.

The daises which he had careful bent his stiff back to pick on this walk to visit his wife's grave lay flat by the base of her stone, the centre of their heads a bright yellow surrounded with a corona of white petals, their assembly connected to long green stems .

He took a step forward, almost a stumble, then placed his hand on top of the old hard granite of the grave stone.

With his head cast down he said his farewells for the day to the plot of ground where his dead wife was buried four years prior, 'back tomorrow again same time Maude?', he asked pausing as if for expecting an answer, 'Nothing planned my dear?' he answered for her, 'Then it's a date.'

'I think perhaps daffodils next time, you do like yellow my love and these sunflowers just don't seem to want to grow anymore without your loving touch.'

He kissed his finger tips then gently placed them on the top of the stone. 'Sleep with the Angels my love.'

The old man turned slowly holding on to the top of the headstone for balance as he did so, a manoeuvre effortless for the young but more cumbersome for a man of his advanced age.

A sloping meadow surrounded by a fence overlooked onto the graveyard and there stood an old mare by the name Rose.

She patiently waited. watching the elderly man approach from where he had been standing, where he had leaned against the big grey stone for the past couple of hours, his back bowed with age.

Rose's breed was a quarter horse, at the ripe old age of thirty-five she was well in her twilight too, the equivalent in horse years as the old man was on his own mortal scale.

She'd watch him ponderously come to the cemetery to visit his wife's grave every day around this same time for about four years now and each time on approach he would first come to the fence where Rose would stand waiting then give her a big shiny red apple that he would delicately polish to a gleam first with a clean cotton handkerchief from which the apple had been wrapped in before handing it to her which she gently plucked from his palm before slowly setting about to munch with her tired old jaws.

After his graveside vigil was finished the old man would head back down to the gate with his rickety gait then stop over by the fence again to where Rose would be waiting for him for the rub he would give her with his grizzled old hands on her threadbare old neck.

The schedule was daily and like clockwork.

The old man would arrive every day late in the afternoon, stay by the stone for a couple of hours then leave before an early dusk as was his routine.

If Rose has a watch and a wrist on which to wear it upon, not forgetting the means to turn the crown on it's side to keep it wound up, then she would have been able to set it by him such was his regular punctuality.

'Well that's another day almost over Rose.' he announced when shuffling up towards the fence where Rose was waiting tentatively.

The old man was careful with his foot placing as he approached the fence as the grass was longer there and put up some resistance to his steps.

He held the fence post for balance upon arrival then leaned forward to caress Rose's long neck which the horse presented to him by leaning her head over the fence.

'Maude send's her greetings to you also this fine evening.' he said.

Rose closed her long lashed eyes such was the enjoyment of her neck being rubbed and her comfort in the company of this old Gentleman she was so fond of. Although she could not understand his words she took comfort from the softness in which he spoke them to her.

'When I get home I shall heat myself that big bowl of the broth which I made this morning. It will warm up these auld bones and stick to my ribs before I call it an evening and get into my bed.'

'Then tomorrow, when I come I shall have the most beautiful bountiful big cardinal red apple for you to munch on Rose, it's nice and ripe awaiting by the widow at home this very moment just biding it's time before it's appointment with your ivories to chomp it my dear.'

Rose gave out a snort of happiness as if to indicate she understood what the old man had just said.

'Yes Rose, tomorrow same time same place. I'd best be getting home now my dear and you best be getting up that meadow to yonder barn and rest for the evening, we both ain't getting any younger and it's me that needs his beauty sleep the most with my whirled auld complexion.'

Another snort from Rose as if it were a laugh with perfect timing.

The old man bid his farewells to the watching mare then started to make his way home for his homemade soup which awaited him on the hob.

Rose recalled when she first met the old man, four somewhat years back now. She observed him from a distance the first time, standing up there by that short standing stone in the field he always visited.

He was wearing a dark suit with a black tie she remembered during her first sighting of him, and there was also that other man present, him with his white dress down to his ankles reading out of a book he held up in front of him.

Rose was familiar with the man in the white dress, she'd seen him often in that field and always in company, never alone. She thought he must make people very sad with what he reads aloud as they all pass through the gate afterwards with tears in their eyes and holding each other wailing with sorrow.

She was glad she was not close enough to hear what he read out, there was enough sadness in this world without inviting more.

That day four years ago there was only the old man there with that same reciter of the book standing close to the stone looking down into at a big hole in the earth.

She could see there were also some casually dressed men wearing dungarees and leaning against spades, it were these same me who dug the hole earlier that day and were awaiting to fill it in again. Rose remember this was what happens from her past sightings of similar times.

They would watch the goings on from a distance, probably not wanting to get to close and hear what the man in the dress was reading or they maybe would succumb to sadness and tears too.

Once the man in the white dress was finished after reading from his book some more she could see the old man bending with a little difficulty to scoop what she believed to be a handful of the soil then toss it in the hole that he had been standing over with his head bowed.

She has saw this many time in that field before, crying people throwing in handfuls of soil into the holes whilst the man wearing the long dress looked on with that book of sad tales held in his hands. Very strange behaviour which she never understood.

Perhaps they were feeding the big seed that they'd just planted in the hole minutes before. Well they were wasting their time as she saw similar big seeds planted a plenty in that there field but nothing ever grew from them and she could always see the people who came back to check on their own sown seeds later. They were always very disappointed at the results as she would then often see them cry and touch the big stone which marked the spot where their seed was planted.

The old man was like that at first too she remembered, when he came each day since the sowing.

He'd stopped crying after a while as she had witnessed but still would stand there patiently talking to the seed, perhaps trying to encourage it to sprout, cox it to grow.

The seeds which they planted in that field looked mighty strange Rose thought to herself. She'd been in her meadow neighbouring to the field since she were but a filly and always a keen observer of the comings and goings in the world around her but she never ever saw that huge seed sprout.

Within the other adjacent field at the top of the pasture which she was in she'd often watch the farmer sow seeds after her big friend Charlie the Clydesdale helped him plough the ground for the seeds. The farmer scattered the seeds into the field by the handful, they were teeny tiny compared to the gigantic seeds which were planted in the other field.

She's like to see the farmer try and scatter these other seeds by the handful she snorted, he'd need big Charlie to help him lift even one of those gigantic pods which she'd saw getting planted under the watchful eye of the man in the white dress, thankfully the farmer here decided to opt for the smaller seeds and a good choice too as they always appeared to grow and did not need a big stone marker for him to remember where he stuck them.

Across in the other field, that one with all the stone markers in the ground, the holes were so deep she'd always note while watching the men with the spades dig them. They'd climb into the holes to dig deeper and eventually she could only see their heads bobbing as they neared the end such was the depth of their burrowing down.

But they were might big seeds right enough, thought Rose, they'd will need a big deep hole. They must be about eight hand spans from top to bottom and a couple wide them there seeds must be, and they came in different colours.

Most were brown as was the one which the old man watched

getting sowed these years ago, then there were white ones too and even ones which looked like the wicker basket the farmer's wife carried the turnips to the barn in, but longer and thicker.

Sometimes she saw a smaller seed getting planted, smaller compared to the other seeds planted in that field but still humungous by what she saw sown in the other field.

These scaled down seeds in these deep holes must really disappoint even more when they don't grow as there always seems to be an increase of the tears and emotions surrounding them during their sowing and still later during the inspections to check if they'd sprouted. Thankfully these smaller seeds appeared to get planted rarer.

T'was all a big mystery to Rose, as was the barn on the hill from where she saw the seed leave to come down to the field to get sown. It was like a ritual, they must be a superstitious lot.

The man in the white dress would walk in front reading from his book of sad verses whilst usually some men behind him carried the seed on their shoulders to the hole.

Behind these men were usually another group of people who always seemed dressed out in black and polishing their eyes like the old man did with that delicious red apple before giving it to her.

That man in the white dress must have been reading from that book in the barn before they left she suspected, as most of the people accompanying the seed were sobbing with tears running down their faces which they would wipe away with their hankies.

Some of the women wore a black cloth which hung down over their faces. When she saw this she would be reminded of her friend Max, the big Belgian Black who lived on the farm next door.

Made her think about when she saw him all fitted out with his blinkers, but Max's were at the sides of his head, these ladies had theirs down over the front of their faces, how did they see were they were going? Perhaps following the noise of that man in the white dress as he read from his sad book.

Sometimes she would hear singing coming from that big barn on the hill when the wind carried it down in her direction. Could it be possible that they were trying to put up resistance and drown out the voice of the sad book she wondered.

A little time before the singing started she could hear bells ringing, perhaps it were cows returning to the farm up on the hill, if so then they must be mighty big heifers as these bells were loud, but it were only once a week and surely too early for the cows to return home. Unless they wanted to hear the singing, she'd heard cows were quite partial to a little bit serenading.

It was mostly on the same day each week as Charlie the big Clydesdale had the day off and was resting in the meadows but on other occasions it were before they set off to sow one of these big seeds.

She would try and listen to these faint singing voices, it reminded her of when the farmer's daughter was younger and would sing to her whilst twirling her mane, she had been but a young filly herself then.

She looked back fondly on such times.

She scarcely saw the farmer's daughter these days now, only from a distance up at the big house but the little girl had all grown up and had moved away with her own two legged stallion.

Sometimes they'd came to visit the farmer pushing a very strange and small looking carriage or carrying in their arms what Rose believed to be their even stranger looking little filly but then again that was some time ago too thought Rose admonishing her old memory for not being so sharp on details.

Now young Max the Belgian Black, a posh one if ever there were with all these aires and graces above his station.

Well he was often directed to go and transport these big seeds from the supplier to the big barn on the hill.

They'd dressed him up all nice, brushed his coat until it shinned and then fitted him with dark black tack and that blinker then stick big plumes on the top of his head which would stick up like tall black ferns, what a sight! How goofy he would look to her.

He then would be harnessed onto a beautiful elegance black carriage which he was to pull.

Max would crow to her that it were a very important job he was required to do by hauling that big seed in the back of the dark carriage, people would walk behind him whilst he led the way.

Sometimes they would stick flowers on top of the seed, decorate it with a little colour for its brief transportation.

The sides of the carriage were glass so when Max pulled it through the village people would see the big seed inside then stop and lower their heads and the men folk would remove the hats there were wearing. Rose wondered if they did this because they knew the disappointment that would follow once the seed was planted and nothing grew from it, an anticipation of such was to be the wasted efforts.

The men who sat on the carriage wore tall black hats and always looked miserable. Max believed it was their expectation of soon having to go into that barn on the hill with the seed then having to listen to that man in the white dress reading from his sad book.

Well Max may think he is something specially getting all dolled up to pull the giant seed to the barn door but Rose considered him not above the rest of them. Just still a drey horse at the end of the day, and he looked a fool with that tall feather sticking up from the top of his head when she saw him all dressed up. More a fool than a goof she decided there and then!

Just as Rose in the meadows was contemplating the strangeness of the goings on in the graveyard the old man had just reached the door of his home, an ivy covered cottage just off the lane which led into the village.

The front garden which was once a sea of sunflowers reaching up towards the sky, a sight which use to warmed both Maude and the old man's hearts but was now just unkept long grass overgrown with brambles and weeds.

The daisies and daffodils with which he would ornament the soil above where she rested were picked on his way to the cemetery during his daily trips. He would bend holding his lower back for support with one hand and pluck the flowers from the ground with the other.

Opening the door and entering the cottage he was greeted with an now too familiar emptiness, that same emptiness which was in his heart since Maude's passing four years ago.

He bided his time in the house now until he was to be called up to take his place with his Maude, the sooner the better he always thought to himself, he missed his wife so profoundly.

The house felt so empty without her there, what value is life without his true love to share it with, the colour faded from the world since she was taken from him.

He could remember her teasing him when he would enter after working in their small vegetable patch.

Look at your trousers! You have more soil on them knees than what's out there in the garden, she would joke wagging a fist but without threat.

Go wash yourself before you are mistaken for a tinker and I'll heat you a nice bowl of warm chicken soup to warm you up.

The words still echoed around his head and threatened to moisten his eyes as he walked into the room to light the lamp as to chase away some of the gloom.

He had some difficulty focusing to touch the wick with the flame from the match due to the cataracts which clouded his old eyes but soon it were lit proper producing a glow around the room.

There! Is that not better? A wee light to see my man's face by and find his hand to hold, he recalled Maude's voice in his memory, by jolly how he missed her! He wished he still had her hand to hold within his.

The old man always thought he would go before Maude and since wished he had been taken instead as the vacuum left in his heart from her parting was like a chasm. He suffer so much from the loneliness and had no other family to comfort him in his grieving.

They had tried for children when they were younger but it were not to be, the stork may have flew over the roof of their little cottage but never made a delivery.

Although it was not a tragedy since they had each other and into old age they grew together in their little abode which was in these blessed days surrounded with sunflowers, and with a love which never faltered that warmed their souls when they were together.

Sitting side by side during the evenings Maude would do her sewing, often stitching patches onto the elbows and knees of the old man's clothes which were always quick to be worn through with his time in the garden or spells during the woodwork which he enjoyed in the little hut down the bottom of the garden.

'Whatever shall I do when the man comes a calling to take you upstairs?' Maude would ask looking at the old man referring to them not getting any younger.

'I think my heart would burst before you were out this cottage door feet first then we could perhaps get a two for one deal with the undertaker,' she would continue.

'Stop this nonsense old woman,' he would reply, 'I have bequeathed it in my will for you to take up with a younger lover and see out your twilight without a cold bed.' He would jest this in reply but the melancholy of these thoughts would hang in the air which was the undeniable fact was they were not getting any younger and one of these day the inevitable would surely happen.

But when the man did come a calling it was not for the old man to be taken "up the stairs", it was for Maude and this broke the old man's heart.

The sunflowers in the front garden just seemed to wither and die after that day when Maude passed away as did the old man's resolve to life.

The old man never again felt the joys of being alive as he had done when Maude was with him, after her death he felt that he only existed.

He got into a routine to make his days pass. Wake up when the light shone in through the window, then to sleep when the darkness came instead. In between he would break his fast with a simple meal of bread and butter which was washed down his age stiffened gullet with a cup of strong black tea, after that he would go about slicing some vegetables and soaking lentils with rice in preparation for the soup which he would then make.

The resulting broth would be for his lunch and later his dinner, then later still, the scrapping left before bed, leaving the pot to soak as to be repeated the following day. A bland concoction more for sustenance than enjoyment.

The only gardening he gave concession to these days now was the attempts to grow the sunflowers at Maude's grave but like the prospect of his life without his wife, this felt futile and pointless with no results to be achieved.

He has lost much weight since Maude died. The clothes were loose and his belt notched tighter around the waist.

He was just skin and bones these days. The furrows on his face were deep and many, his joints knotted and back crooked.

The vegetable patch in the back garden, which was once his pride and joy had since overgrown with weeds as like the front garden. He could never muster the energy to work in it again since her passing.

He use to walk into the village twice a week to shop at the store and get some bread, butter and the vegetables, these same vegetables which once he would grow in abundance in his garden but not anymore.

He would also buy some of the reddest apples with Rose in mind, the thought of that old horse and giving her the apple sometimes felt as if that was what was keeping him ticking over these days, the push in his mind to make him move.

When he walked into the village some people would say greetings out of politeness yet that generation never knew the old man's name and there would never be any other dialogue exchanged apart from brief salutations and short polite comments about the weather as he stood in the queue in the store to be served.

These outings soon came to an end when he found out that he could get the young boy who stocked the shelves in the store to deliver his staples twice a week to the cottage.

The boy would knock at his door, place the basket over the threshold, just inside once the door opened then take receipt of payment from the old man and a few coins extra given for the boy's troubles.

The boy liked the old man and thought he looked like he had tales to tell but he could also sensed the air of sadness about him so again only the briefest of pleasantries were exchanged during these deliveries.

The old man had lost all delight in his world without his beloved Maude he thought to himself. No, that's not quite true he corrected as he looked across to the big red apple sitting by his window. I take a pleasure from when I see Rose at the fence awaiting me as I visit my Maude each day.

That was true, each and every day since his Maude was placed in the ground he would visit the old mare at the fence which separated the meadow from the graves.

Once upon arriving he'd greet her fondly then give her the big red apple which he would always carry in his pocket wrapped in a clean cotton hanky be brought along for that very purpose. Then once leaving his Maude before returning home he would again go over to Rose at the fence and give her a good old rub on her neck which she seemed to love.

He tried to remember how he knew the horse's name was Rose but his old memory would not help him. Perhaps he just gave her that name himself one day, could have been in association from the rosey red apples he would feed her?

She did look like a Rose he thought, a beautiful Rose to brighten up the otherwise darkness of his life when he passed through it.

He did not know much about horses before meeting Rose.

His only prior experience was when accompanying Maude on a Tuesday afternoon to the Regal once in a while to watch a John Wayne or Gary Cooper cowboy flick over some shared popcorn. Or sometimes when crossing the street to avoid the drey delivering barrels to the alehouse which he used to frequent in town for a quick half lemonade shandy when Maude was preparing their dinner back at the cottage during which now felt like another life.

He'd certainly never been up close to a real live horse before, they looked big powerful beasts and he'd heard they could bite a harvest moon size lump of flesh from your leg if they were to take a dislike you you so he always had a fear, yet he still could not fathom what drew him towards Rose.

Four years ago, that day when he put Maude in the ground, the old man had hobbled back towards the cemetery gates taking his leave with salty tear tightened cheeks and wearing his black suit and tie.

The priest, who had been the only other person present during his Maude's laying to rest had read the committal pray from the bible as the old man had tossed a handful of soil into the grave landing on the top of her coffin with a dull thump before the gravedigger moved in to fill the hole.

The priest, after a few personal words of condolence to the old man parted his company then returned up the hill to his church, an opposite direction to that of which the the old man would take leaving the graveyard.

Just before he had headed out of the gates the old man saw the horse intently watching his journey from near the graveside exit where the boundary fence separating the cemetery from the farm meadows next door.

He had stopped and stared back at the horse who just continued to stand there, large head looming over the fence looking at the old man with interest.

He had shouted 'what?' towards the horse as if asking to what was the horse staring at and expecting an answer whilst lifting up both his hands palm towards to the sky in exclamation.

The stand off had continued, neither dropping their stares.

The old man then lumbered up towards the horse, his shoulders heavy from carrying his grief and back bent already from the burden of life.

When a couple of feet away he looked closer at the old horse, looked into her eyes, eyes which were almost as cloudy as his were, and was astonished by the intelligence and compassion he saw there. He'd never saw such feeling in the eyes of another soul, animal or human since his wife's departure, or for that matter of it, over these past four years since.

He did not expected anyone to apprehend the true measure of the pain he was feeling within his heart that day but this old mare seemed to perceive some of it.

The Priest with his "Go with God" certainly did not inspire, but there, in the least likely of places where he would have expected it, there he felt the strange sensation of someone understanding him.

The pale blue eyes which started back at him through the opacity of cataracts, similar to what clouded his own vision these days, appeared to be knowing his suffering and had empathy for it.

He then, without the slightest trepidation reached both hands out to the horses muzzle and held them there close to her nose. She appeared to read the old man down to his very soul then she would allow him to caressed her with these same old arthritis warped fingers to which she responded with a purring like sounds as her long lashed eyes changed into a dreamy like cast, the bond was established.

The pain in the old man's heart felt a little more abated then at that very moment in time, it never quite disappeared but he felt, with the understanding which appeared to emanated from the large animal, that he could manage the grief just enough to get through this heartbreak, take it one day at a time, and that be did.

His heart did remain ruptured with his loss but the sight during the following days of that old horse watching and waiting for his arrivals, then awaiting him still as if to wish him farewell on his departures during his visits to Maude's grave, it drip fed him just enough love each day as to carry on through his suffering.

For these first couple of months immediately after the death of his beloved Maude, the old man had considered many times to expedite his reunion with his dear wife.

In his frail state i would not take much he thought.

It could be after dark, a little stroll out to the woods then a walk into the middle of the duck pond, he thought almost feeling the cold water around his legs with the abstraction in his head. The green algae coloured water would only reach past his waist but then if he were to drop to his knees, just allow them to buckle as they often felt like they would do, just to succumb to the weight from the yoke of sorrow which he carried, then he knew he would never ever get up again and soon find his peace.

He'd also, some evenings during his darkest period, look up at the rafters in his little cottage's ceiling and wonder the possibility of climbing up on the table to loop his trouser belt over one such rafter and the other end around his auld scrag of a neck then drift his feet off the edge of the table, swing with that final step and end it there.

Or down the bottom of the garden where the hut stood within which he had once worked with wood as Maude was in the kitchen. One of these snaggletoothed saws could go through wrist better than it could wood he thought, then he could just sit down, arms presented at each side of his body and wait for his life to drain out.

But during these bleakest of moments there was the strangest of thoughts in his head with broke through the dark like a ray from the sun and that thought was that if he was not around tomorrow then who would bring Rose her shinny red apple the next day and such was his reason to meet with a new dawn.

After a lunch of soup and crusty bread the old man set off again on his crippled gait alone along the path toward the cemetery to visit his Maude…and Rose which he would surly tack onto the end of his thoughts about Maude, which were his simple agenda for the day.

The big ripe red apple wrapped in a fresh clean white cotton handkerchief in the pocket of his overcoat for Rose to munch down upon.

On his way he stiffly bent to pick some wild daffies from the side of the road. You will love these Maude he thought to himself, beautiful yellows and greens, a gift for you my dearest of loves.

There was the gate in sight and the fence at the side with Rose waiting as was she would do for the past four years.

What a warming sight for sore eyes thought the old man with the only other smile to crack his face when not reminiscenceing about his late wife.

He could see Rose's excitement as he approached. She soon settled and he got the big apple from his pocket. He could hear Rose snort her approval upon its sight.

'Big, ripe and juicy,' he declared of the presented fruit, 'especially for you Rose.'

He gave the apple its habitual polish with the hanky then balanced it on his outstretched palm toward the horse folding his gnarled finger joints under it.

"There you go my auld girl," he offered, 'let's feed this apple as I can see you have been waiting patiently for this here treat.'

Rose gently plucked it from his shaky outstretched hand then lifting her head back she crunched it with extreme satisfaction.

She made light work of the apple, pips and all.

The old man caressed the side of her flexing muzzle as she chewed eliciting soft wheezes of gratification from the horse's nose as she eat.

"Well I'd better not dilly-dally any longer my dear and go get myself over to see our Maude, she'll be expecting her daffodils now, and see the pretty one's I picked for her," he said holding up the posy of daffies level with Rose's face to show her.

Again Rose snorted in approval.

"See you on my trip back my dear." And with that the old man slowly turned and walked along towards Maude's grave for his daily respects.

Rose, with the delightful juices from the munched apple dribbling on her droopy lips, watched the old man totter away towards were he would stand by the plot in the field. She so very much wished that the seed would germination for him, it had been four long years but the man did not seem to lose faith and was still very patient waiting each and every day by that stone marker, looking at the ground there for the sign of a shoot to sprout from the earth.

With the years that passed since their first introductions he seemed forever getting more bowed and dawdling with his walk, she knew this was the signs of his age and felt a great sympathy for him.

How she dearly wished that reason for his visits would sprout soon as Rose knew it would give him such happiness.

Rose wondered if the old man felt lonely, she'd only ever saw him by himself.

She once had a partner, a beautiful stallion called Blaze, and a Blaze he was under the sun galloping around the field.

He was at first kept in a separate paddock from her she remembered. Then the farmer and one of his brothers would bring Blaze into her paddock for a visit during which time he would mount upon her back and plough her she remembered with a fondness, and that seed Blazed did sow had sprouted, unlike these others in the the field neighbouring to her paddock she'd thought.

She remembered feeling the seed Blaze planted into her, its tap roots moving in her belly as they took hold.

The farmer would keep coming across to her poking and probing checking on the progress of the germination then one evening when the farmer was there with another, a stranger she never met before, on that evening she could not get comfortable and had to lay down.

Then out soon sprouted an immediate bloom, a divine little foal to who she felt such an attachment. It was to shakily stand to its unsteady legs to which she felt an immense pride to watch.

She missed that little horse that had came from the seed which Blaze had planted inside her.

He was taken from her by the farmer after just after a year and she never saw him again but there was some compensation to be had as shortly after during that same year Blaze was to join her in the field again although he never was to attempt and plough her once more so no more seeds to make little horses somewhat to her regret but his company was much enjoyed just having him close to her.

He did not seem as angry as he once when he would see others over the fence in the other paddocks, and so he was a more amiable companion keeping her company there as they would stand close together and chew the grass.

Blaze was older than Rose, she remembered. She watched how his back started to dip and his hairs went grey down his face as the years past, just as Rose's was now.

He had developed a hollow look in his eyes and took longer to get to where their oats were served.

One day she remembered he would just want to lay down all the time and that was when the farmer knelt beside him stroking his side and then that stranger came again, the one she'd first saw when the little horse sprang from her.

Rose was led away from Blaze that day by the farmer. She was taken far down further away along the meadow and when she returned later to the barn Blaze was no longer there nor was she ever to see him again after that. She felt a profound sadness at the memories of the loss yet still there was an ember of happiness with the recollection of Blaze and their time in the field together.

The old man approached his wife's grave. As he bent he placed the daffodils at the foot of the headstone, the daisies were still looking fresh from the day before so he rearranged them slightly to accommodate the freshly picked flowers at their side and as he was down there he checked the soil where he always planted the sunflower seeds but still nothing.

Perhaps the earth is too stony he thought to himself again, a deliberation that ran through his mind often these past few years, as were the other rationales, too dry, too wet, too shallow or deep or not enough sun.

He felt exceptionally tired this day, he felt tired every day but on this recent walk from the little cottage to the graveyard he felt even more so and had to stop a couple of times on his journey to rest.

On one of these pauses the old man had sat on a bench situated at the base of a mighty oak overlooking the duck pond which was void of any ducks.

The boy who delivers the old man's groceries was returning from a recent delivery pulling a small cart behind him when he saw him seated there just looking off into the distance.

The boy decided to go and sit next to him for a moment, check that he was alright.

'Good afternoon Sir,' the boy politely greeted the old man, 'it's a lovely day is it not?' he asked.

It seemed to take the old man a moment before realising the boy's presence there sitting beside him on the bench as if he were awaking from a trace.

'Ohhh, hello young man,' he then answered, 'yes, it certainly is a fine day, I was just commenting upon that very thing just now to my Maude'

The boy was somewhat taken back by this as the old man appeared to be alone, but then the boy knew how kooky the old can be sometimes. He had a grandfather, albeit not as elderly as this old gentleman he sat beside but still some of the things he would say appear very odd.

'Have you been off on your errands?' the old man continued as then noticing the cart parked off to side of the sitting boy's legs.

'Yes Sir' the boy answered, 'I have just been to deliver some provisions to the Father Thomas up top of Cemetery Hill.

'I deliver there each morning but I was a bit later today. The Father likes his eggs and a quart of milk to be delivered fresh each and every day.'

'Ahh, that is the direction I am headed in. Did you see my Rose over there during your travels?' inquired the old man.

The boy again found this an odd question but respectfully replied 'No Sir, I don't know anyone by the name Rose and never met a soul on my way there. Only you Sir on my return back.'

The old man seemed to look off into the distance again. The boy was about to take his leave but then the man addressed him again.

'Have you ever been in love my young friend?' he asked seemingly out of the blue.

Normally the boy's face would redden with a blush at such a question but there was a sincerity and trust when in the company of the very old such as the person who he was sat there next to, so the boy answered straight and honest with only the slightest hint of the blush of embarrassment.

'Yes Sir, there is this one girl I really like. Her name is Mary and she works down the draper's store. She is so pretty and always smiles when I see her.'

'Do you give her flowers?' asked the old man.

'No Sir, well…well maybe, maybe sometimes. If a see a daisy on my trips, if I see some on the ground, in the grass, I sometimes pick one, or maybe a couple or even a few then I hand it to her when I see her,' this boy paused a moment looking into the old man's face and felt a sincerity of interest there so he continued, 'She pucks the petals off one at a time whilst saying "he loves me" on a petal's extraction as it floats to the ground, then on the alternate ones she says "he loves me not". It always finishes with "he loves me!' the boy beamed whilst recalling this, his face then going even more crimson with the recounting.

The old man smiled in return then said approvingly 'That's good young man but you must also give her flowers to show that you remember!'

'Show that I remember what Sir?' asked the boy curiously.

'To remember you both, to remind each other what love is,' replied the old man then continued on, 'and give her sunflowers to show that you worship and adore her with all your heart.

'Show her the unwavering faith and unconditional love that you have in her.

'A sunflower's face will follow the sun across the sky as your heart will follow your true love no matter what and that is why sunflowers are the very best flower to remind each other what true love is about.'

The boy asked 'but there are no sunflowers in the fields for me to collect, only wild flowers and daffies.'

'Then you must grow your own my dear boy, plant the seed, grow then take its offerings to your loved one to show her that your heart is true.' After saying this the old man slowly raised himself to his feet. The boy also stood and offered the old man support getting up.

'I must be on my way young man' he said, 'in the absence of sunflowers I must pick some daffodils on my way to see my Maude and I have an apple for my good friend Rose who will be awaiting my arrival by the fence so I must bid you farewells.'

At this the old man slowly walked back onto the path and started out again in the direction of the cemetery.

The boy stood and watched the old man shuffle slowly away, bent with age and looking older than ever.

He had enjoyed his brief exchange with the old man, there was a certain comfort he felt speaking with him. Normally he would never have told anyone about Mary but he the old man felt like a confidant to him, someone he could tell his inner most and not feel judged, ridiculed or have his trust broken. It was a rare feeling, and there was a certain warmth in the advice the old man had parted to him. The boy told himself that he would indeed pick some wildflowers after dropping off the empty cart back ay the store, then he would go and give them to Mary, show her the love he felt just like the old man had said. He also then made a pact with himself that he would purchase some sunflower seeds and plant them out in his ma's garden, in the ground on the spot when the sun shines so brightly during these long days, yes, that's what he would do then soon he would have some sunflowers to in his hands to give to Mary, such was the influence of what the old man had advised him.

* * *

The old man trudged across to the fence where Rose awaited eagerly, he hobbled across with his increasingly curving back.

'There's my girl!' the old man announced as he reached Rose at the fence whilst unfolding his handkerchief to extracted the apple then giving it its customary polish before handing over to the horse presented on the palm of his hand.

'Another red apply delivered from my old hands for your delight.'

Rose with slow precision gentleness plucked the bright red apple from his offered palm with her teeth.

'You like your apple my girl,' he said, 'these past years we have became good friends girl have we not?'

The horse snorted as if in agreement whilst crunching on the received apple.

'I don't know how many of these here trips I have left in my old bones but the pleasure of seeing you at that fence each afternoon has gave me my reason to have kept going and that I can't ever thank you enough for my dear Rose.' The old man had turned his head during this sentence and stared across the graveyard toward's Maude's headstone.

Rose could not understand exactly what the old man was telling her but she felt the emotions radiating off him.

There was a melancholic sadness to her friend, especially more so that day. She could feel it emanate from him like steam from the dewy grass under the heat of the sun.

She felt very affectionate toward the old man, she sensed he had a good heart the way only animals can sense such things. He was lonely but with a good soul.

Each and every day he would come and check on the seed he had planted in the field next door these four years ago when they first met but still nothing grew yet, she could sense his waiting although sometimes she could not quite determine if it were a waiting for the seed to grow or waiting for something else but if so then she never knew what.

The old man looked again at Rose, focusing his milky catalytic eyes to her face and spoke 'Sometime my Rose, sometimes I believe you understand me, read my heart as only one person in my life did once before.

'You would have likes my Maude and she would have loved you

my dear. My Maude was the gentlest creature on this god's green earth.' The old man folded the handkerchief as he spoke.

'She had the patience of a saint with me did my Maude. We used to go everywhere together and whilst walking side by side our hands would dock into each other's like as naturally as the bee attracts to the flower.

'When I worked in my woodshed or the garden I sometimes could hear her rattling pots and pans in the kitchen, just that awareness she was in my life would keep my heart afloat.'

The old man went quiet for a while as his eyes stared off into a memory then the horse nudged him gently on his shoulder with her muzzle as if to prompt him to continue which he did.

'True love is rarer than floating stones Rose, and I was blessed to find such a love with my Maude

'Oh I was not perfect, we could argue. She would throw her arms up in the air with frustrated irritation at times and declare me to be the biggest cretin when I would trudge muddy footprints going in from the garden across the kitchen floor which she had just newly cleaned and I would oppose her complaints telling her that I was exhausted to pay attention to such trivialities but even then my heart was still full of love for that lady.

'Sometimes we don't appreciate the blessings we have do we Rose? We take for granted that the sun will raise every morning and the moon will follow telling us to get on up to our beds.

We just always believe they will be there and I believed Maude would always be with me, then one day she was not.'

Rose continued to listen to the old man. Although she did not understand what he was saying she knew he was expressing something from deep within him and as such she understood the sentiment. Her fondness of this kindly old man keep her rooted to the spot with her full attention eager to be of help even if all she could do was to be there for him and listen.

'Maude's favourite colour was yellow' the old man went on, 'she would stop too look at the yellow lichen on the trees, or freeze with delight when a yellow warbler would land close to her on a tree branch.

'She loved wild daffodils too but what were her very preferred flower was the sunflower, she use to say that the sunflower signified unwavering hope and unconditional love.'

The old man places his hands tenderly on the horses face rubbing her fur as he continued.

'Do you know the story of Clytie and Apollo, Rose?' he asked the horse rhetorically then waited a few seconds as if for an answer before continuing.

'Clytie was a young water nymph who was in love with the Sun God Apollo in the times of mythological Greece.

'When Clytie died the God Apollo turned her body into a sunflower. Her love for him was so very true and strong that once reincarnated as a sunflower she would then watched him move across the sky every day in his sun chariot. Just the same as sunflowers follow the sun, this was her true love for Apollo.'

Rose listened intently as the old man spoke. When in each other's company it was as if something would transcend the equine to human barrier. Although words which passed through the old man's lips onto the air Rose could never understand the meaning of, she did comprehend the emotions behind the dialogue.

The locution of tones and expressions of his face and body language which rendered a great grief and sadness coming from the old man and in turn Rose felt such love and compassion for him, for this kindly old fellow who would hobble across to the fence and speak to her with such an affection and always have an apple to present her with.

Over the years she would see her friend getting older, his back more crooked, his amble increasingly laborious, yet never once did he fail to make that journey across to the fence each and every day to give her a shinny red apple and kind words before going across to the other field to check on his planted seed where there he would stand for a while then on return approach Rose by the fence again to bid her farewell until the next day.

'Maude always told me', the old man continued, 'that when her time came she would like to be brought back as a sunflower, tall, proud and with a straight back with her face up towards the sun.'

The handkerchief he'd earlier used to wrap then polish the apple with he now used to dab at tears forming in the corners of his eyes.

'I miss her, I miss her so very much Rose.' With these last words the old man slowly turned and made his way painstakingly slow towards the cemetery gate to continue onwards towards Maude's grave.

* * *

Once the old man had finished his respects by his wife's grave he again, as was their custom, bid Rose farewell with a goodbye rub on her nose as he gripped the fence post for his balance.

The next day Rose waited patiently by the fence to see the old man approach but she never saw him and could not understand why.

She was perplexed by his absence. This was the first time he had missed during the past four years.

Rose never saw him the following day either or the one after that.

A couple of days later, during the morning, Rose noticed some activity going on in the field where the big seeds were buried, sometime happening at the plot where the old man would visit.

Two men with spades were digging another hole right beside it, slightly to the left of where the old man had sown that big seed these years ago.

Later that day Rose saw yet some more happenings around that freshly dug hole which she had watched being excavated that same morning.

There was one of these big seeds getting lowered by ropes, lowered down by these same two men who had dug the hole earlier.

There also was that man in the white dress again and a boy she recognised, that same young lad who pulled the cart behind him up to that barn on the hill every morning.

After the seed was planted the men started filling the earth with soil. Rose wondered what the old man would think about this seed being planted so close to his, yet still she had not seen him now a few days. Where could her dearest friend be she wondered.

The young boy left the cemetery.

He was sad that the old man had passed away and sorry to notice that he was the only person who was by his graveside at the burial apart from the grave diggers and the priest. It was not much to show for a life time on this earth.

When he had heard the old man had died he was very sorrowful, he wished he had got to know the old man much more. The stories which the old man could tell would now go untold thought the boy who would never hear them.

As he left through the cemetery gates pulling his empty cart behind him, then he remembered he had one last thing to do.

Across he walked to the fence where the old horse was watching him.

He left his cart behind as he walked the last few steps to where the horses head was extended over the fence.

'Hello', the young boy said, 'You must be Rose.'

Rose regarded her visitor, she'd often seen him from a distance walking passed pulling that cart of his whilst making deliveries.

She watched the boy reach into his pocket and pull out a big red apple.

He was about to hand it to her but then paused for a moment as if in thought.

He then pulled out this shirt tail and started polishing the apple with it, getting it nice and shinny then offered it to Rose on the palm of his flat hand.

Rose continued to stare at the boy for a moment longer, then decided on trust so gently retrieved the offering from his palm and started crunching the rosy red apple.

Rose continued to wait by the fence for the old man to appear but he never did. She missed him terribly and longed to see him once more.

Her new daily visitor appeared. Every day in the mornings for the past couple of months the boy pulling his cart would stop by and go over to the fence to greet her. Just like the old man did.

The boy would have a juicy big red apple for the horse which he would polish with his shirt tail before offering it to her.

He was a very kindly boy, Rose could sense this in him very well and started to grow fond of his daily morning visits.

One sunny morning Rose looked across at the neighbouring field, the one with all the upright stones and was surprised to see something growing on plot of ground which the old man would attend on his visits.

Rose was amazed as to what she saw.

Two of these massive seeds had finally spouted!

Out of the grass, which now grew brilliantly green on top of the filled hole which the men had lowered the big seed a couple of months ago, were two tall thick stems with large green leafs.

Up upon the tops of these tall stems were their crowning glory, large flowering faces with bright vivid yellow petals around their blooms, and their heads facing towards the sun.

Such a beautiful sight to behold and finally something has at last grown from these big seeds thought Rose.

If only her dear friend the old man was here to see this wonderment, she just knew in her heart this would make him very happy, very happy indeed.

The two sunflowers stood there side by side reaching up proudly toward the heavens just inches apart on top of the pair of the graves.

ALSO BY DEARN SAVAGE
Available on Paperback and Kindle
MEMORY BOXES

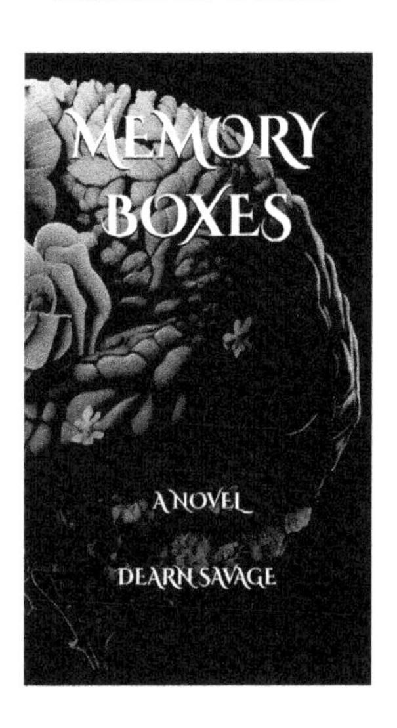

Daniel Sinclair escapes within memories to diminish his torment whilst awaiting the inevitable at the bedside of his dying mother Annie who's once treasure house of a mind has since been pillaged bare by the ravishes of dementia brought on by her Alzheimer's disease.
His estranged young son Sam stashes away his own remembrances of his loving father as if it were contraband to be hidden from his embittered mother Lilian.
Hope has all but left Daniel, that is until Maria enters his life. With a devoted love she tames Daniel's dragons, changing them into harmless butterflies and in doing so teaches him to believe and dream again. But he also must make peace with the past as not to allow it to destroy his future.
This is a journey of birth, death, love and forgiveness as hope is rekindled and actions taken to regain the traction needed to find a fresh zest of faith and with it the chance to reunite with his son after years of being apart.

Printed in Great Britain
by Amazon

26772121R00071